"Get out of my office."

Jumping to her feet, Bethany pointed to the office door.

"But…"

"No buts. I'll speak with my *dat* and have him straighten this out. He'll be in touch."

"Be in touch?" Aaron asked.

"*Ya*. You heard me. Now shoo."

"I'm not a horsefly, Bethany."

She stomped around her desk, opened the door and motioned him out.

And to her surprise, he went, but before he did, he stopped right in front of her, his eyes a mixture of annoyance and humor and something she couldn't quite identify. Worry? Maybe fear?

"I wasn't supposed to report to work until Monday," he explained. "I just wanted to get the lay of the land."

"Not necessary, since you're not working in my RV park."

"I'll see you on Monday, when your *dat* told me to report to work—here, at this office."

"We will have whatever this misunderstanding is cleared up before Monday. Trust me on that."

Vannetta Chapman has published over one hundred articles in Christian family magazines and received over two dozen awards from Romance Writers of America chapter groups. She discovered her love for the Amish while researching her grandfather's birthplace of Albion, Pennsylvania. Her first novel, *A Simple Amish Christmas*, quickly became a bestseller. Chapman lives in Texas Hill Country with her husband.

Visit the Author Profile page at LoveInspired.com.

Her Amish Adversary

Vannetta Chapman

LOVE INSPIRED
INSPIRATIONAL ROMANCE

LOVE INSPIRED®
INSPIRATIONAL ROMANCE

PLEASE RECYCLE
THIS PRODUCT IS RECYCLABLE

Recycling programs
for this product may
not exist in your area.

ISBN-13: 978-1-335-58548-6

Her Amish Adversary

Copyright © 2023 by Vannetta Chapman

For questions and comments about the quality of this book, please contact us
at CustomerService@Harlequin.com.

Love Inspired
22 Adelaide St. West, 41st Floor
Toronto, Ontario M5H 4E3, Canada
www.LoveInspired.com

Printed in U.S.A.

Let the peace of God rule in your hearts.
—*Colossians* 3:15

Love is friendship that has caught fire.
—Ann Landers

This book is dedicated to my Amish friends.

Chapter One

Bethany Yoder directed Oreo to turn into the southeast entrance of the Shipshewana Outdoor Market—*The Largest Market in the Midwest*, as the banner so proudly proclaimed. Her *dat* was the owner and general manager of the market. Her family was Amish, which meant that pride was generally frowned upon. When it came to advertising though, a little bragging was allowed.

Oreo tossed her head, as if she were looking forward to visiting the small field next to the RV park. Oreo was their older mare, and Bethany thought she was the sweetest thing on their farm. She still pulled a buggy just fine, though they'd often find her sleeping on her feet when she had to wait. Bethany parked the buggy in a sunny corner of the unpaved parking area. Setting the brake, she hopped out onto the ground, fed Oreo a carrot from her pocket and wound the reins around the hitching post.

"Less than an hour." she promised, then turned toward her office.

Her office. Who would have thought that those two little words could bring a person such joy? She'd initially resisted the job as RV park manager, but she had found in the last few months that it suited her perfectly. Once she'd accepted that she liked what her *dat* had wanted her to do, she set about making the little office into her personal haven.

She'd sewn gingham curtains for the windows. Knitted pillows to put on the small couch. She'd even crocheted a rug for the floor, which had been a real learning experience. Working with a large ten-millimeter crochet hook wasn't for the faint of heart, and using strips of fabric instead of yarn had been awkward at first. The result, though, had been stunning— an oval-shaped multicolored rug. Now her office felt as if it were truly her private domain. With four sisters, she was used to sharing space. Working in the little office building had shown her how special a space of her own could be—though of course guests were encouraged to visit her there.

She smiled when she even thought about her little office, and she loved going to work five days a week. She rarely went in on Saturday and never on Sunday. This Saturday was the exception. Earlier that morning, her oldest *schweschder*, Sarah, had discovered she needed a few items from the grocer, and Bethany had readily volunteered to go.

Her plan was to spend an hour, maybe two, in the office, then pick up the items on Sarah's list.

Two hours alone in her office. She practically skipped down the path that led to the small building.

The sun was shining after a week of rain, the weather forecast promised the day would warm to the mid-fifties, and Bethany Yoder was happier, more satisfied, than she'd ever been.

She stopped twenty feet from the small front porch of her office building. It was technically a chalet shed, built by the Amish there on the property, with gray plywood siding, a dark gray shingled roof and a white-trimmed waist-high railing around the porch. The door had fifteen rectangular panes of glass, which allowed plenty of sunlight to stream into the single large room. She'd placed her desk under the double windows that were set off with dark gray shutters from the outside.

It was like an Amish dollhouse, only life-sized.

Why was the door ajar?

Frowning, she cautiously crept forward. Should she go for help? Or should she investigate on her own? Surely she hadn't been robbed. And even if she had been, no doubt the thief would be long gone. She glanced down, and her eyes widened at the large muddy boot prints that led up the single step, across the small porch and into her office.

As she entered the fourteen-by-eighteen-foot room, her eyes were on the muddy prints tracked across her newly crocheted rug, so she didn't immediately notice the man sitting at her desk. He'd pivoted the chair away from the desk and was looking through her filing cabinet.

She let out a startled scream, and the man jerked around, nearly toppling over her lamp in the process.

"You gave me a fright there, Bethany."

"Aaron? Aaron King?"

"For sure and certain. It's been a long time, *ya*?"

Not long enough, Bethany thought. Somehow she managed not to voice that uncharitable response. Aaron looked as he'd always looked, though perhaps more handsome than before. His rolled-up shirt sleeves revealed arms that were muscular and deeply tanned. Why did Aaron King have a tan in April? Then she remembered he'd been living in Sarasota, Florida. So what was he doing here? In Indiana?

She glanced around the room and tried to think of a single reason why Aaron would be in her office. She couldn't come up with even one. "What are you doing here? Why are you sitting in my chair? And what were you thinking tracking mud across my new rug?"

Aaron cocked his head and smiled apologetically. It was quite maddening. He was maddening, as he'd always been.

"I'll answer the last question first and work my way back. Let's see." He leaned back in her chair and ticked her questions off on his fingers. "Sorry about the rug. Didn't notice. I'm sitting in your chair because I was trying to find a roster of what guests are in which RV sites, and I'm working here."

"I need to sit down."

"*Ya*, you're looking a bit peaked."

Bethany collapsed into the guest chair in front of her desk, let her purse drop to the floor, propped her elbows on the desk and massaged her temples. This couldn't be happening. It was—literally—her worst nightmare. She opened one eye hoping that Aaron had disappeared. No chance. He waved at her.

He actually waved!

That was enough to make her blood boil. Bethany was usually a quiet, even shy person. She rarely kicked up a fuss, only voiced her opinion when directly asked to do so and went out of her way to avoid confrontation. Aaron King sitting in her chair behind her desk after tracking mud through her office changed all of that.

"You will be taking my rug outside and cleaning it—cold water only. I just finished making it last week."

"It's a rug. Aren't people supposed to walk on it?"

"It's a hand-crocheted rug, and the sign that I hand-embroidered and posted next to the front door says, 'Please wipe your feet before entering.'"

"Huh. Didn't see that." Aaron shrugged. "Sure. I'll wash the rug."

It had always been that way with him. A complete dismissal of others' concerns—an air that said, *You're being silly, but okay.* It was infuriating. Aaron was infuriating. He had been infuriating for as far back as she could remember.

"As for who is in what site—not that it's any of your business—I keep an up-to-date chart on the whiteboard." She jerked her head to the right.

Aaron's eyebrows arched in surprise, then he stood and walked over to the wall. Bethany used the moment to dash around the desk and reclaim her seat, reclaim her place. As Aaron studied the names on the board, Bethany studied him.

Still sturdy like an ox—no doubt as stubborn as one too. Probably five foot ten. Could that be right? Yes, he'd grown at least two inches since their school days, and he'd been taller than her then. She'd guess his weight at 185 pounds—all solid muscle by the looks of things. Sandy hair that was a bit too long at the collar and nearly fell into his blue eyes completed the picture. He could be a model for one of her *dat*'s tastefully done advertisements—that thought only upped her irritation.

When he turned back toward her with that boyish smile, all of the times that he'd teased her came rushing back. She wanted to stand and stomp her foot. She wanted to tell him to get out of her office.

Instead, she placed her palms flat against her desk and measured her words. "Aaron, there must be some mistake."

"I don't think so—unless you have another RV park here at the market."

"My *dat* hired you?"

"*Ya.* Yesterday."

Her *dat* had been at the market the day before doing interviews for the coming season. He'd come home late and left early for a horse auction in Goshen. He and Gideon—who would be her *bruder*-in-law in less than two weeks—had been quite excited about buying another horse. She hadn't had a chance to ask him how the hiring had gone. She hadn't thought to. She didn't pay much attention to what happened in the rest of the market.

But what happened in her domain was another matter. Why hadn't he told her?

Aaron was still waiting for an answer.

"We don't have another RV park. This is the only one, and I'm the manager."

Aaron shrugged and flopped into the chair across from her. "Maybe he thought you needed help."

"I don't."

"Then maybe I'm supposed to replace you."

Bethany was usually a very calm, mild-mannered person. She rarely lost her temper and always took time to process her emotions. But when Aaron said the words "replace you," she actually saw the color red.

Jumping to her feet, she pointed to the office door. "Get out."

"What?"

"Get out of my office."

"But…"

"No buts, and leave the rug. I'll clean it myself."

"Fine by me."

"I'll also speak with my *dat* and have him straighten all this out. He'll be in touch."

"Be in touch?"

"*Ya.* You heard me. Now shoo."

"I'm not a horsefly, Bethany."

She stomped around her desk, opened the door and motioned him out.

And to her surprise, he went, but before he did, he stopped right in front of her, stared down at her—his eyes a mixture of annoyance and humor and something else she couldn't quite identify. Concern? Worry? Maybe fear? None of that made any sense. She'd never been good at reading people's expressions, and today was no different.

"I wasn't supposed to report to work until Monday," he explained. "I just wanted to get the lay of the land."

"Not necessary since you're not working in my RV park. How did you get in anyway?"

"The key was under the flower pot, where everyone puts a spare."

She held out her hand, palm up and waited. With a roll of his eyes and a shake of his head, Aaron pulled the spare key from his pocket and dropped it into her hand.

"So, I suppose I'll see you on Monday, when your *dat* told me to report to work—here, at this office."

"We will have whatever this misunderstanding is cleared up before Monday. Trust me on that."

For one brief moment, she thought he might reach out

and tweak her *kapp* strings. Fortunately for them both, he simply shrugged, put his straw hat on his head and walked out into a beautiful April morning.

And that was when she figured it out.

Today was April 1. Her *dat* always had been a joker. This was all an April Fools' joke, and she'd nearly fallen for it. She'd thought that Aaron was serious and that her entire life was about to be turned topsy-turvy. That probably wasn't the correct expression. It was probably something her *schweschder* Ada had said—Ada, who misquoted every saying.

Regardless, she breathed out a sigh of relief. An April Fools' joke she could handle. Aaron King in her life was another matter. She would clear this up as soon as she saw her *dat*. They'd have a good old laugh over it. So what if she had to spend a half hour scrubbing her rug? It was on the floor of her office—her private office. That alone was enough to cause her to hum as she fetched a bucket of water and a brush.

Aaron walked back across the market grounds with his hands stuck in his pockets and his head down. He tried to imagine how things could get any worse, but he came up blank. He was back home in Shipshewana—the last place he had expected to be. He had accepted a job at the market—the last place he had expected to work. And now he'd learned that the one girl he hadn't been able to forget from his school days was his boss—or at the very least, his coworker.

Bethany Yoder was hardly a girl though. She'd grown into a beautiful woman. That must have happened while he was in Sarasota. She no longer resembled the plump little girl that he'd looked forward to teasing every day.

She was taller, nearly reaching his shoulder. And she had turned into something the *Englisch* magazines might describe as curvy. Same brown eyes studying him though. And when he stepped close enough, like when he'd stood in front of her and returned the key, he'd been able to make out the familiar light spattering of freckles on her cheeks.

He kicked a can that was rolling across the sidewalk.

Bethany Yoder.

She was a year younger, but he'd always been tongue-tied around her. Intimidated by her, if he was honest. She was smart and kind and everyone liked her. She had several *schweschdern* older than her and one who was younger. In other words, she came from a normal Amish family. He'd felt envy and attraction and confusion all at the same time.

Which was probably why he'd teased her so much. He hadn't known how to act around girls then. He still didn't know how.

He was so busy scowling at the sidewalk and kicking the can that he almost ran over James Lapp.

"Hey, Aaron. I'd heard you were back."

"*Ya*. Where'd you hear that?"

"You know how it is. Someone told someone who told someone else who told my *schweschder*. I think I heard it from her."

James was also a year younger than Aaron, but in a one-room schoolhouse, everyone had known everyone. Aaron wondered briefly if James and Bethany might be dating, then decided it wasn't any of his business. James fell into step beside him as he continued toward the green parking lot where he'd left his bicycle. He didn't even have his own horse and buggy. It was embarrassing.

"What are you doing at the market today?" When Aaron didn't immediately answer, James waved at the empty stalls. "It's not as if you're shopping."

"I just took a job here."

"Seriously?"

Aaron tried to put his best spin on it. It wasn't as if he could tell the truth. "My parents are friends with Amos—"

"Oh, *ya*. Everyone's friends with Amos."

"They'd heard he was hiring."

"It's a *gut* place to work, and Amos—he's strict, but he's a fair boss."

"Do you work here?"

"This'll be my second year as an animal auctioneer. Where did Amos put you?"

"RV park." He again kicked the can. "I didn't even realize they had an RV park."

"It's a fairly recent addition. Gideon, he's the assistant manager now and also he's marrying Becca, though that's an entirely different story. Anyway, Gideon started the RV park in the winter, before Becca came back. I think he was trying to work extra hours so he wouldn't worry about Becca so much."

"I don't know what you're talking about."

"Becca and Gideon were sharing the position of assistant manager, but you know how Becca always wanted to leave—to travel."

"*Ya*, she used to talk about it in school."

"Exactly. The problem was that those two fell *in lieb* before she could go. We all recognized the signs before they did. Then Becca went off on a MDS mission…"

"Mennonite Disaster Services?"

"The same, and while she was gone, Gideon started the RV park. Like I said, he was trying to stay busy is my guess."

Becca Lapp was marrying? She'd never seemed much interested in dating or settling down. Everything had changed. Aaron didn't mind being back home as much as he hated that nothing was the same. What was the use in coming home if everything was going to be different than before? On the other hand, it irked him that so much looked as it did the day he left—things like Main Street and his parents' farm and the market.

He was annoyed by both the changes and the lack of changes, which proved he was in an irritable mood.

"Whatcha chewing on over there?"

"Bethany wasn't too happy to hear that I'd be working with her."

"Ah."

"Ah, what?"

"No one expected that of the five Yoder girls, Bethany would come to work here at the market. She always seemed shy and kinda uncomfortable in crowds."

"Can't say as I noticed that."

"Then she started working at the RV Park and took to it like a Labrador takes to water."

"She seems to think she owns that office."

James laughed good-naturedly. "I think we have a good team here, and we pull together when necessary."

"But?"

"But when it's not necessary, everyone has their own area. It'll make more sense to you after you've been here a while."

Aaron didn't know about that. He had no idea if he

would be here for a while. His future—his family's future—was a large black hole in his opinion, and thinking about it caused his head to hurt.

They'd reached the green parking lot, and he nodded over to his bike. "This is me."

James didn't even comment on the bike. Of course he didn't. Bikes were the thing in Shipshe. Sort of like the three-wheeled adult tricycles that were so popular in Sarasota.

"I'm walking over to the coffee shop to meet my *bruder. Gut* seeing you."

"*Ya*, you too, James."

As Aaron pedaled home, his mood improved.

First of all, he knew that he was right—Amos Yoder had hired him to help run the RV park. So there must have been a need for him there. Which meant that whether Bethany wanted him there or not, it was his job.

Secondly, he was good at working on RVs. In fact, he was great. Sarasota had seemed like the RV capital of the world to him, and he'd found that he was quite adept at fixing things that went wrong with recreational vehicles. RV problems to him were like a crossword puzzle that made sense.

Then there was the money aspect. He'd done the math with his *bruder* just the night before. The bank had given them an extension of six months. Ethan would work the fields and take care of the animals. If anyone could make the old neglected place profitable, his *bruder* could. Aaron would bring in money from working at the RV park—the hourly wage that Amos would pay him and hopefully additional money on the side from doing upgrades to folks' RVs.

Amos had made him a good deal in that regard. Any

work done while Aaron was on the clock would be billed and paid to the market. Any work done on his off days or after hours—mainly building sheds, porches or closet space—would be paid directly to Aaron. He didn't know how much that would be, but he knew that he was adept at the work.

Between the money he earned and the money from the crops, they might be able to pay the bank enough to receive another extension. And in a year, maybe two, they might actually be out of the hole his father had dug.

Thinking of his *dat* caused him to stop pedaling and coast as he turned onto Huckleberry Lane. Aaron hadn't seen his *dat* yet, and he didn't want to. Of course, he would help his *mamm*. Of course, he would do the responsible thing, but that didn't mean that he had to greet his father with open arms. Zackary King had done more to harm his family than help. He was a selfish, bad person. Aaron had accepted that years ago. He would stay on the old farmstead and help, but he'd only do it for his *mamm*.

As for being back in Shipshewana, he didn't mind so much. It had been a *gut* place to grow up—not too big, not too terribly small, though the town itself was tiny. The market had always been the center of things and attracted huge crowds. Shipshe would be an okay place to live. It was just that after seven years in Sarasota, he felt as if he'd come home with his tail tucked between his legs. As if he'd done something wrong.

But he hadn't.

He'd moved on with his life as his grandparents had counseled him to do.

He'd grown up and learned to be independent.

He'd put some of the nightmares of his youth behind him.

And now he was back. He'd work at the market as long as necessary, save up his money, help his *mamm*. Once she was financially stable, maybe he could move to Goshen or Elkhart. He had no burning desire to go back to Sarasota, but he didn't want to live with or near his *dat* either, and the man would be back home eventually.

Setting things right should take one year, two at the most.

He'd just have to remember to keep his muddy boots off Bethany Yoder's rug. As he pedaled into the family drive, he laughed, because she'd looked so cute when she had ordered him out. Let her assume that he was barging in and trying to take over. As long as she didn't guess the truth about his family, about how bad things really were, he didn't care what she thought.

Or at least that's what he told himself.

Because the idea of Bethany Yoder feeling pity for him was absolutely more than he could bear.

Chapter Two

Bethany directed her mare Oreo toward the front of the house, set the brake, hopped out of the buggy and jogged up the front porch steps to drop the bags of groceries in the kitchen. When she walked back out onto the porch, she noticed Gizmo lying in a patch of sunlight. Gizmo was an old farm dog of undetermined age. Bethany thought he'd been around since her second year of school. He now slept away most of the day. She knelt to scratch him behind the ears. "Special treats after dinner. You have my word on it."

Gizmo sighed contentedly. Bethany promised Oreo she'd be back to unharness her soon, then she hurried over to join her family at the fence of the east pasture.

Becca's betrothed and her *dat* were in the field with the new mare. All of her *schweschdern* were standing at the fence—watching and calling out encouragement.

"She's a beauty." Bethany crossed her arms on the top rail of the fence and glanced to her left and right at her *schweschdern*. As usual, they were standing in birth order—something they laughed about but still always did. Sarah was the oldest at twenty-nine. Their *dat* had stopped trying to set Sarah up on dates, often murmuring, "Perhaps *Gotte* will bring the right man to our front door."

Becca came next at twenty-four. Since she'd come back from her mission work in December, she seemed to have matured years beyond her age. She was still pleasant and optimistic. At the moment, she was smiling at her husband-to-be or the horse or maybe both. But she also had quieter moments when Bethany couldn't tell what she was thinking about…perhaps the families that she'd helped on her mission trips.

Eunice was next in line. She was twenty-two and was the mechanical one of the sisters. Like today, she usually had grease on her face or hands. She looked over at Bethany, then at Oreo and then back at Bethany. With a smile, she said, "We've been watching for a half hour. You stay, and I'll take care of Oreo." Eunice was like that—always the one to jump up and do something that needed to be done.

Bethany was next. She and her younger *schweschder* Ada were the youngest—they'd been quite young when their *mamm* had died.

Ada was the baby they'd all coddled and taken care of, though now she was nineteen and hardly in need of babying. Ada had trouble settling down—with a boy or a job. She was nearly done with her yearlong commitment at the local schoolhouse, which her *dat* had insisted she keep when she wanted to quit midsemester. It wasn't that Ada was lazy, only that she had a very short attention span.

"Her name's Kit Kat, and I can't believe she's going to be ours." Becca glanced at Bethany, smiled, then turned her attention back to the reddish-brown horse. "Aren't her black tips amazing?"

Indeed, the mare was black on her tail, mane, legs and the tips of her ears.

"She's a beauty, for sure and certain." Bethany was happy for her *schweschder* and all of the exciting changes that would come in her life. She was rather glad it wasn't her though. She liked for things to be the same. She'd be a bundle of nerves if she was about to be married, was leaving on a trip in two weeks and had bought a new horse. That would be a lot to process, though it didn't seem to be bothering Becca one bit.

Gideon had put a halter on Kit Kat and was attempting to lead the horse around the pasture. The horse stopped on the opposite side of the area and stubbornly refused to move. Instead, it cropped at the grass pushing up through the dirt.

"It's just like they say…" Ada sighed. "You can lead a horse to a pasture, but you can't make it keep walking."

Bethany, Becca and Sarah all shook their heads and laughed, but no one corrected Ada. It was rarely worth the effort to explain to Ada how she'd misquoted her sayings.

It was hard to believe that they would have three mares now—Oreo, Peanut, who was the youngster on their farm, and now Kit Kat. More horses was a sure sign of a growing family in Amish communities. Bethany tried to picture all of them married and living on the family farm. They'd need to enlarge the barn.

"Your mare is beautiful, Sis." Sarah wrapped an arm around Becca's shoulders and squeezed. "But I have chores inside that will not get done on their own."

Sarah seemed surprised when Bethany joined her as she walked back to the house.

"How was your trip into town?"

"*Gut.*"

"But—"

"I didn't say 'but.'"

"*Nein*, you didn't, but it's written on your face." Sarah hooked her arm through Bethany's. "Tell me all about it."

So she did. As they unloaded the groceries, scrubbed the potatoes, seasoned the chicken and placed it in the oven, she spilled all the details. About Aaron appearing in her office. Aaron claiming he was there because her *dat* had hired him. She left out the part about the muddy boot prints because it sounded a little petty.

By the time she was done, they were sitting out on the porch with a cup of tea and a tin of homemade granola.

"Do you think it could be an April Fools' joke?"

"Sorry, but no. It isn't. He mentioned hiring Aaron to me when he came in last night. I think you were already in bed."

Bethany's spirits sank like a popped balloon. Of course it wasn't a joke. Her *dat* wouldn't do that. "I suppose Dat hired him yesterday and hasn't had time to tell me."

"They left early this morning for sure."

Bethany frowned at her tea. "I don't need help at the RV park though. I'm doing fine on my own."

When Sarah didn't answer, Bethany glanced up. "Aren't I?"

"Well…" Sarah reached for a handful of granola and popped some in her mouth. After chewing and swallowing, she continued. "You were at a loss as to how to handle the black water / gray water problem last week."

"I don't even know what that is."

"And you weren't about to go into site eight's trailer and help them catch a mouse."

"Nope. Not in my job description."

"Maybe those things are in Aaron's job description."

Bethany set her chair to rocking, frowned and considered Sarah's words. Sarah never was one to sugarcoat things—except for food. The granola had been dusted with brown sugar and was quite good. Finally, Bethany sighed, reached for a handful and said, "*Ya.* I see your point, but I don't like it any better."

"What's really bothering you? I don't think it's just the fact that you'll have to share your office."

Bethany visibly shivered at that, then told Sarah about the rug, which caused her *schweschder* to laugh. "Aaron only has the one *bruder.* His house probably wasn't filled with handmade rugs."

"I guess."

Sarah didn't push. She'd been eleven years old when their *mamm* had died from cancer. She remembered her *mamm* better than any one of them except for their *dat,* and she'd fallen into the role of caring for her younger *schweschdern* quite naturally. She seemed content, but Bethany wondered if she truly was. Would she remain single until each one of them had married? That might be a long wait, as Bethany couldn't think of a single candidate for her, or Eunice either. Ada would probably marry before the rest of them. Ada was adorable and easygoing. She'd have laughed at mud prints on her rug.

Bethany stared out across the farm and broached

what was really bothering her. "I don't suppose you remember Aaron from our school days."

"Pretty sure I was out before he was in. There must be eight years between us. I do remember his older *bruder*, Ethan. He was a quiet, serious kid. When they finished school, both boys moved away? Right?"

"I think so." Since Aaron was a year older, Bethany had enjoyed one year of school without his teasing. By that point, though, she'd become shy and quiet and didn't know how to act any other way.

"Aaron made my life miserable back in those days. He teased me constantly, and I didn't know how to react. I didn't know how to stand up for myself, so I just tried to hide in the schoolhouse if everyone else was playing outside. Even at church, he would tease me. I'm telling you, he made my life miserable."

"I'm sorry, Bethany. I never knew that."

"Some days I even faked a stomach ache, though actually, the stomach ache was real now that I think about it. I'd have gladly chosen a cold or a toothache or a stomach ache over being teased all day."

"It was that bad?"

Bethany shrugged. "I understand it was only kids being kids, and I suppose I made a *gut* target. Other girls might laugh with him or tease back."

"But you didn't."

"Nope. I was too timid then." She tried to smile at this not-so-different image of her younger self and failed. Instead, she took another sip of her tea. "Not nearly as outgoing as I am now."

"The fact that you are not outgoing isn't a mistake. *Gotte* made you how you are, Bethany. Embrace that."

"And how do I do that?" She swiped at a single tear.

What a silly thing to cry over. What was wrong with her? Why was she so sensitive? And how could she create a tougher outer shell?

"Realize your quiet nature is not a mistake or a defect of any kind. Try thanking *Gotte* that you do care so deeply about things. And maybe give the people around you—even Aaron—a break."

"Easier said than done."

"No doubt."

"It's not as if I have much choice. I can either cry every day…" She wiped away another traitorous tear. "Or quit the job I love or…or get tougher."

"I don't know that it means getting tougher." Sarah reached over and patted her hand, then began gathering up their things. "But you could try to see the humorous side of things."

"Like boot prints on my rug?"

"Exactly."

Sarah kissed the top of her head, on top of her *kapp* actually, causing Bethany to feel five years old again. Then she went inside, leaving Bethany there to consider her words, process her emotions and decide how she was going to face the next week. Because the one thing she was sure of was that she was not going to quit her job.

She loved her job, and she was willing to fight for it if that was what was required. She might even be able to learn how to catch a mouse, though she suspected anything to do with gray water was beyond her. She had skills though. She made visitors feel comfortable, made them feel as if the RV park was their home away from home. That was worth as much as the ability to fix plumbing problems.

* * *

Aaron's *mamm* had dinner on the table by the time he and Ethan had finished with the day's chores. His *mamm* was a *gut* cook, and he was starving. Thick slices of ham, baked potatoes with fresh butter and cheese, corn and okra—all items that Bishop Ezekiel had brought over from his own supplies. Esther hadn't kept a garden the year before, the family's milk cow had been sold to cover debts, and they certainly didn't have any pigs. Still, the food was *gut* and Aaron was hungry.

They bowed their heads for a silent prayer, then began passing dishes.

Ethan talked about the south field. They didn't have a work horse, so he'd hitched up their mule to the plow and turned the soil over that way. It had taken twice as long as it should have, but the job was done, and a portion of their crop was planted.

Aaron shared that he'd gone to the market and checked out things at the RV park. He didn't mention his run in with Bethany Yoder. No need to bore them with that.

Finally, his *mamm* cleared her throat and pushed her plate away. She'd eaten less than half of the food. Esther King was only forty-three years old, but she looked older and frailer than she should have. She looked like twenty-five years of marriage to their *dat* had worn her down, and Aaron suspected they had.

"I spoke with your *dat* this afternoon."

Both Aaron and Ethan set down their forks and waited. Aaron attempted to steel himself against more bad news.

"He's feeling much better. The doctors are trying a new medication—"

"And since he's there, he has to take it." Aaron regretted the words as soon as he'd said them. "Sorry. Go on."

"Yes, he has to take it. That's a condition of his staying at the Health Center. At this point, he's sleeping a lot. I'm going to see him next week. Bishop Ezekiel has arranged for Jackson to pick me up on Thursday morning."

"Jackson's still giving rides to the Amish, is he?" Ethan laughed and resumed eating. "Remember that old Cadillac he had? The seat covers were torn and the paint job was faded, but that engine was a thing of beauty."

"He now has a van." His *mamm* pulled her coffee cup toward her and wrapped her hands around it. "Or so I've heard. I haven't had a ride with Jackson in years."

Neither Ethan nor Aaron had a response for that. They'd both fled the family farm—fled their father— as soon as they'd graduated from the local one-room schoolhouse. Ethan had gone to Ohio to live with cousins and learn how to properly farm. Aaron had opted to stay with his *mamm*'s parents in Sarasota. While they were becoming men, their *mamm* had continued dealing with their *dat*.

She was still dealing with their *dat*.

"I'm bringing it up in case either of you would like to go with me."

Aaron thought the top of his head might explode. "The last thing I want to do is visit him. He's the reason we're in this mess. He's the reason that you are nearly homeless."

His *mamm* didn't respond. Esther King was very good at not responding—she'd developed it into an art form. But the look of misery in her eyes immediately caused Aaron to regret his outburst.

Ethan, as usual, was the one to smooth things over. "You're right, Aaron. *Dat* is the reason that the farm is in such poor shape and the reason that we owe the bank—"

"Not just owe it. The payments are past due."

"*Ya.* I was with you both when Mrs. Garcia explained the terms of the loan." Ethan finishing cleaning his plate by mopping up the last of the baked potato with a crust of bread. Pushing back from the table, he crossed his arms and studied them both. As the oldest son in the family, he was naturally the one to take their *dat*'s place. Ethan was only twenty-four, but many Amish men were married with a family and farm of their own by that age.

"*Mamm* did the best she could while we were away."

"I know that."

"And what *Dat* did, it wasn't entirely his fault. This mess we're in…it's a direct result of his bipolar disorder."

"It's a result of his refusing to take his medication properly. *Mamm*, why did you hide it from us for so long? Why did you let things fall into such a bad state before telling us? Before telling anyone?"

He thought she might start crying again, but Esther was tougher than that. She sat up straighter and pushed her coffee cup away. "Perhaps I should have, Aaron. I waited as long as I could because I hoped things would improve."

"And yet you knew they wouldn't." Probably he should have held those words inside too, but he was tired of letting all of his anger and resentment fester. He needed to give voice to the thoughts circling in his mind, or he feared he'd explode.

"I did." She nodded and finally met his gaze. "I knew

they wouldn't get better, but I'd hoped to buy you both enough time to become men. And you have. I'm sorry that I need your help now. I wish I could have thought of another way—"

"We don't mind helping, *Mamm*." Ethan looked to Aaron, who nodded in agreement.

A part of him did mind though.

A large part of him had wanted to stay in Sarasota, create a life there and never look back.

"*Gotte* has provided me with two *gut* sons, a compassionate bishop and a husband that I truly believe can get better." She pushed on before Aaron had a chance to voice his doubts. "Just because that hasn't happened in the past doesn't mean it won't happen at all. Faith is believing in things not yet seen, *ya*? It is the very essence of things hoped for."

"Sure, *Mamm*." Aaron stood, pushed in his chair and carried his dishes to the sink. "Now I best go and brush down Misty."

He heard Ethan continuing to speak to his *mamm*, but Aaron couldn't handle one more second of the conversation. Twenty minutes later, Ethan joined him in the barn. By that point, Aaron had mucked out the stall and checked the mare's hooves. Misty didn't need grooming every day, but she had received a thorough brushing every day since Aaron had returned. It was one of the few things that calmed his irritation.

"She's still a *gut* mare." Ethan retrieved the comb and began working it through her mane.

"Old like everything else around here." Aaron couldn't help laughing when Misty nudged his hand. "But *ya*, a *gut* horse."

"Remember when *dat* first brought her home? You were what…six?"

"Seven. I thought she was my birthday present." At that age, he hadn't accepted that birthdays were a minimal affair at their house. He'd still dreamed of that extra special surprise gift.

"My point is that *Dat* did some things right. Misty here, she was right for us."

The horse was gray with a black mane. That mane was now mixed with gray as well, her teeth were worn down, and she spent most of her days dozing in the sun. But she was a *gut* horse. She had always been a *gut* horse, and she could still pull a buggy. Aaron placed one hand flat against her side and brushed her coat with the other. He and Ethan finished her grooming together, then put fresh oats in the bucket and walked out into the cool spring evening.

"Do you regret coming back?" Ethan's voice held no judgement.

"I regret that she needed us to come back."

"You don't have to stay."

"I'm staying."

"We can make this right, Aaron. With your job at the market, and my work in the fields—we can do it."

"We can if he won't interfere. But what do we do when he comes back from the Health Center? This farm isn't only suffering from neglect. The things he didn't do are bad enough, but he also sold everything that wasn't nailed down."

"And probably some things that were," Ethan admitted.

"I have no doubt that he would have sold Misty if

he'd been offered any money at all for her. At this point, she costs more in upkeep than she is able to deliver."

"She's still a *gut* horse."

"Indeed."

Ethan nudged Aaron's shoulder, and some of the tension in Aaron's body melted away. They closed up the barn and walked back toward their home, stopping a few feet shy of the porch. In the last of the sun's fading light, they studied the place where they'd grown up. The house was in need of painting and reroofing. The steps were a hazard. One window had been broken, and cardboard had been taped over the hole.

When they'd arrived, there had been scarcely any food at all in the pantry and no propane gas for the stove or the refrigerator. Aaron couldn't imagine how his *mamm* had managed to hide her poverty from the rest of the church...or why she'd chosen to do so.

Ethan pushed his hat back. "I'll admit that the circumstances of our return aren't the best—"

"That's an understatement."

"But we can do this, Aaron. And it feels *gut*. It's satisfying to bring a place back to life."

"*Ya*. It might be. If he doesn't come home and start the downward spiral all over again."

"We won't let that happen."

"I'm not sure we'll be able to stop him."

And there it was—his biggest fear. What if all of this work was for nothing? What if the pattern from his childhood repeated itself yet again? And how was he to have faith that this time could be different when everything he'd experienced taught him that it would be the same?

Those troubling questions followed him into the

house, back to his room and tormented him as he tossed and turned throughout the night—occasionally interrupted by images of Bethany insisting that he "get out."

Chapter Three

It was probably a good thing that they didn't have church Sunday. Bethany was not ready to see Aaron King again. Instead, they shared a meal with Gideon and Nathan, the old guy who Gideon had lived with since moving to Shipshe from Texas. It was hard to believe that Gideon would be living with them in eight days. The wedding was to take place on Tuesday, April 11. Gideon's parents and siblings were riding up on a bus for the event. Everything was changing, and Bethany wasn't sure why life was like that. Why couldn't things just stay the same?

What was wrong with the way things were?

Though, watching Becca, she understood that moving forward was natural and normal and good—at least for other people.

She wasn't a fan of change. She never had been.

Unfortunately, she was going to have to live with the change of Aaron working in her office. Her *dat* had been quite adamant about that. "You need help, Beth." Only her family called her by the pet name. She thought he might be using it now to lower her defenses, but it wasn't working. She tried several different lines of reasoning.

She could do better.

She would do better.

She would prove that she didn't need help.

"You've done a fine job, but you have no idea how busy the market can be in the summer. I'm hoping that will mean the RV park is busier too. Trust me, you'll be grateful for Aaron's assistance."

She doubted that.

There had to be a way to change her *dat*'s mind, but she had no idea how to do so. Maybe Aaron would mess up and get himself fired. Her *dat* did not put up with lateness, rudeness or a bad work ethic. Was it too much to hope that Aaron would exhibit one or maybe all three of those characteristics?

As if to squash her uncharitable thoughts, Aaron was waiting outside her little office when she arrived on Monday morning. Once the market was officially open for the season, they'd shift their days to Tuesday through Saturday. For the next month though, it was a Monday through Friday affair. Aaron sat on the front porch in the single chair under the roof overhang, watching her as she walked toward him.

A light rain was falling and the temperature was rather cold, but Bethany thought it still smelled of spring. She tried to focus on that and not on her nemesis waiting in the porch chair.

"*Gudemariye*," Aaron said, smiling and standing as she walked up the three steps.

She thought of ignoring him, but ignoring Aaron King would not make him go away. She was an adult now, not a young scholar who would have done anything to avoid being teased. She met his gaze. "*Gudemariye*."

He held the screen door open as she closed her umbrella, set it to the side, then dug through her project bag looking for her keys.

Aaron made a big show of wiping his shoes off on the outdoor mat. No doubt he hoped she would comment on it, so she didn't. The last thing she wanted was for Aaron to think that she was happy about his presence.

She walked around the small room, turning on lamps and opening the window shades. Aaron stood with his hands in his pockets, watching and waiting. Finally she pulled out the chair behind her desk and sat.

"Are you going to just stand there all day?"

"I don't know. I was waiting for your permission, I guess." He delivered the last line with a mischievous smile as he sat.

Bethany placed her hands palms down against her desk. "I spoke with my *dat*. He insists that I need help."

"Great."

"Not great. I do *not* need your help, Aaron, but since my *dat* believes I do and since he is the general manager for the market…"

"Maybe it won't be as bad as you think. I can be pretty handy to have around."

"Uh-huh."

"I hope you noticed that I waited on the porch instead of barging into your office."

She closed her eyes for a second, but he was still there when she opened them. Sighing, she opened her desk drawer and pulled out the extra set of keys. She set them on the desk and pushed them toward Aaron. "The spare is back under the flower pot in case you get locked out."

"Wow. My own keys? It's almost as if you trust me."

"I never said I didn't trust you, and you need a key if you're to work here."

Aaron sank back into his chair, leaving the key on the desk between them. "This is all too tense for me, Bethany. Can't we just be friends…like we were in school?"

"Friends?" The word came out sharper than she intended. She lowered her voice and glared at him. "We were not friends in school, Aaron. Maybe you don't remember the time that you put a garden snake in my desk."

"I'd forgotten that, but since you brought it up… Your face turned as red that day as it is now."

"Or the time that you locked me in the outhouse."

"I heard they added actual bathrooms to the school."

"Or how you sat in the back and made faces every time I had to stand in the front and give a report."

"I was trying to help you relax." Aaron shifted in his seat. "Look, that's all in the past. I barely remember anything from those days."

"I remember everything."

"We were just kids."

"So, you're saying you've changed?"

"Of course I've changed." He jumped up and paced the room, pausing to stare at a cross-stitch sampler that read, *RV There Yet?*

Finally he walked back over and sat again in the chair. "Maybe we should start over. Hi. My name is Aaron King, and I'm looking forward to working here in the RV park." He actually held out his hand as if she were supposed to shake it. Instead, she picked up the keys and dropped them in his palm.

"Try not to lose them."

"Aye aye, Captain."

She pulled a folded sheet of paper from her bag. "I've written up this list of things that need to be done."

Aaron accepted the list and studied it. Finally he looked up, his head cocked to one side. "What are you going to be doing while I do all of these jobs?"

"Look. It's a *gut* way to separate chores. You be in charge of the land. I'll be in charge of the tenants."

"Uh-huh."

"I'm more of a people person than you are."

"How do you know that?"

"Because I know you, Aaron. Remember? School days?"

Aaron shrugged. "Okay. But just to be clear, no one said that you're the boss of me."

"What?"

"I'm just saying. When Amos offered me the job, he said I was to *help* you run the RV park, so while I appreciate your list of chores, I'll do what I see that needs to be done."

Bethany squeezed her eyes shut and clamped her teeth together. He made her so mad. He hadn't changed one bit.

Always opinionated. Always right. Always irritating.

By the time she opened her eyes, he was gone.

Hmmm.

She'd have to remember that acting like a child made him disappear. That could come in handy.

Aaron whistled as he walked through the RV park, Bethany's list tucked firmly in his pocket. He didn't need Bethany's list, and if she thought he was going to limit himself to mowing, raking leaves and carrying out the trash, she was in for a big surprise.

He needed this job. There was no way he and Ethan could catch up on the family bills if he didn't do well here. Plus, he was hoping to find some work on the side.

It made sense to start each day by taking a walk through the RV area. A place couldn't be run inside an office. You had to step outside and see things for yourself. Bethany was probably at her desk working on another cross-stitch thingy—at least he thought that was what it was called. That was all *gut* and fine for a *mamm* trying to make a home seem warm and cozy, but this was a business.

As he walked the grounds, he noticed a few tree limbs that had fallen and needed to be carted away. Some were rather large. He'd have to check to see if Amos had a chainsaw. In fact, where were the outdoor tools? The questions lined up in his mind as he walked past each RV, noting the condition of the trailer, whether the occupants seemed to be here permanently or passing through, and what handiwork he could do to improve their visit.

The good news was that there was plenty of space in the park, plenty of room for expansion. The bad news was that it seemed as if very little had been done. Sites had been leveled. Someone had installed electrical and sewer hookups. That was it. There weren't even picnic tables with each site.

He found the storage shed with outdoor tools and took a quick inventory. Spying a pad of paper and pen on the workbench, he began jotting down items he could use. Then he spent the rest of the morning emptying the large trash barrels that were at both ends of each row of trailers. In all, they had eighteen trailers—small by Sarasota standards. But he could envision more. He could envision this being the premier RV resort in Northern Indiana.

As he was making his way back to the office, he noticed an old *Englisch* man untangling his dog's lead rope.

"Nice beagle you have there, sir."

"Pepsi? Yeah. She's a good dog, but she loves chasing squirrels. That's how she gets this leash all tangled up."

"My name's Aaron King. I'm assisting in the running of this RV park now."

"I know Bethany must be relieved to have some help. The last time we had possums in the trash, I thought she was going to have a stroke. I'll admit they do rather look like large rats."

Bethany didn't like varmints? Aha. Aaron filed away that piece of information—could come in handy later.

Aaron knelt beside the beagle, offered his hand palm side up for the dog to sniff, then proceeded to rub Pepsi's long ears. "Are you here for a while or passing through?"

"I thought we were passing through, but the wife has found a knitting club downtown that meets on Mondays and Thursdays. Plus, we've found the people in Shipshe to be quite friendly. I think we'll be staying, at least for a few more weeks—maybe longer."

"If you'd like, I could build a portable fenced area for Pepsi. Probably wouldn't have to be over waist high."

"You would do that?"

"I'd have to charge you for the supplies and the labor. I could write up an estimate."

"That would be much appreciated. I wasn't sure they'd let us put a fence here or who I'd ask to do it."

Aaron shook hands with the man whose name was Gus Whitaker. "I'm your handy guy. Anything you need, just ask."

"I'll do that."

"And I'll have you an estimate by tomorrow."

He was whistling as he made his way back toward the office. He could do this, and just as importantly, he could enjoy it. He'd learned a lot about RVs while working in Sarasota. He'd also learned a lot about RV people. They enjoyed their freedom, being able to easily pack up and move on, but they also wanted to feel connected to a place. Whether they were staying for two nights or a month, they wanted to leave with fond memories and to feel like they'd be welcome when they returned.

Aaron walked the last few feet to the office, opened the door, then remembered the rug. Stepping back outside, he wiped his feet not once or twice but three times. No need to cause Bethany to have another meltdown, though she was rather cute when she blushed to the roots of her hair.

Speaking of Bethany, she was standing in the corner at what looked like a small kitchen making a cup of tea.

"Wouldn't mind one of those myself." Aaron shrugged out of his coat and draped it over what he thought of as his chair—the one on the visiting side of the desk.

"Tea packets are in this box."

"No coffee?"

"Over at the main break room. If you'd like, we could get some instant for here."

She was actually being pleasant. He couldn't believe it. Maybe she'd come to her senses and realized it was a good thing that he was around to help.

"The teas are separated by flavor. To work the electric kettle, simply push down on this button."

He'd moved behind her to see the things she was pointing at. She looked over her shoulder and jerked away in surprise. "Didn't realize you were so…close."

"You're a bit like a cat. Aren't you?"

"A cat?"

"*Ya.* Jumpy."

"I don't think so." She took her tea to the desk and sank into her chair. "How was your first morning?"

"Gut."

Was he imagining it or did that answer disappoint her?

He pushed the button down on the kettle, chose the peppermint tea, dropped it into his mug, then waited for the water to boil. When he'd finished making the tea, which was nice and hot but not nearly strong enough, he sank into the chair across from her. "How was your morning?"

"Fine."

He knew he shouldn't ask, but he was curious. "What did you do?"

"Not that it's any of your business, but I took a couple of reservation calls, ordered supplies for the bathrooms and showers…"

"I was happy to see that cleaning those wasn't on my list."

"Katie does that. Wouldn't want you taking her job."

"Of course not." Did Bethany think he was trying to take her job? He had no desire to sit in an office and… was that knitting she'd been working on? He couldn't imagine taking reservations and knitting all morning.

"I made a list of items I could use to spruce up the place a bit." He slid the sheet of paper across the desk.

"Spruce it up?"

"There are some limbs that should be cut and hauled away. I'm going to need a chainsaw unless your *dat* has one on another part of the property."

"I doubt it. This is the only part with trees." She studied the list, a pout forming on her pretty lips. Finally, she shook her head and said, "You can take it to him. You'd be better able to explain why a wheelbarrow, leaf blower and three flats of flowers are needed to run an RV park."

He thought of defending his list, but the look on Bethany's face said that she plainly did not care.

If Aaron had a lick of sense, he would have stopped right there, taken the list to Amos and gone to lunch. But when had common sense ever directed his steps?

It was more than that though. He liked unsettling Bethany Yoder—he always had. He'd told her that he remembered little of their school days, but that wasn't completely true. He remembered how she'd always had that placid, calm expression. How it had always irked him. She looked as if nothing could surprise her, as if she had the world by its tail, and the world would definitely bend to her rules and regulations.

Bethany had always been a woman who was calm and controlled.

But was anyone really that calm?

He pulled the second sheet of paper out of his pocket, studied it a minute and then held it up. "Great. While I'm talking to him about supplies, I can go over this list of upgrades."

"Upgrades?"

"Sure."

"Why do we need upgrades?"

"Don't you want your park to grow and prosper?"

"My park is fine as it is now. We don't need to grow and prosper. What's on that list?"

"Well, doesn't sound as if you'd be interested."

"I'd like to see it, please."

He gave her what he hoped was a boyish grin. "Well, since you said please..."

And the effect, as she read the list, was exactly what he'd hoped for. The calm expression was replaced with surprise, then disbelief and finally indignation.

"We don't need a community firepit."

"Why not?"

"Or a dog park. This whole area is a park."

"In my experience, guests like to be able to let their dogs run around off leash."

"Complete with a dog-washing station?"

"Very popular in Sarasota."

"We're not in Sarasota, Aaron, and this list...all of this is ridiculous. What would people do with a gazebo?"

"Eat lunch there. Maybe read a book. Just enjoy the day?"

But Bethany wasn't listening. Her frown had become quite pronounced, and she kept stabbing her finger at his list of upgrades.

"You want a place to play horseshoes and a washer pit? What is a washer pit? Never mind..." She shoved the piece of paper back across the desk, picked up her knitting, stared at it, then jammed it back into her bag. "Why don't we just go over together and see my *dat*?"

"Now?"

"Good a time as any, unless you're too busy."

"Fine by me, but I don't see why you need to be there."

"Because this isn't the future that I want for my park."

"Your park, huh?"

"Yes, Aaron—a plain and simple park, not a camping mecca, not a…" She stabbed a finger at the top line on the sheet of paper that listed his ideas. "Not a resort! Amish people don't have resorts."

"It's only a word, Bethany. It simply means there are added amenities. And I wasn't suggesting that we do all of these things at once."

"I don't think we need to do them at all." She stood, snatched her coat from a hook and flung open the door. "Well? Aren't you coming?"

"Oh *ya*. I wouldn't miss this for the world."

Because he was pretty sure that Amos would be on his side. Amos was a business man, and he wanted to provide a good experience for his guests. Bethany was playing house, and she was stuck in the past.

It was a good thing he hadn't mentioned building a fence for Gus Whitaker. That might push Bethany right over the edge. As he jogged to catch up with her, his shoes splashing in the rain puddles, he couldn't help noticing—again—that she was awfully cute when she was riled up.

It was too bad that she was attempting to stand in his way, because that was something that he wasn't going to allow.

Chapter Four

Bethany led the way into her *dat*'s office. He'd just returned from lunch. She knew that because he always brought a mug of coffee back to his desk to tackle the afternoon's paperwork. The coffee was steaming. They'd caught him when he was full and would probably welcome a distraction. Good! She fully expected this to go her way, but she could use any available help to make sure it did.

"This is a nice surprise. I didn't expect to see my *doschder* and my newest employee right after the lunch break." It was then that Amos seemed to notice they weren't there to tell him how well things were going.

Bethany knew the symptoms of when he was bracing himself for trouble. Possibly, it was the way Amos sank into his chair and sighed heavily, as if he couldn't possibly carry the burdens of their jobs in addition to his. She remembered Aaron asking her what she'd done all morning, and her temper flared even hotter.

"Both of you have a seat and tell me what this is about."

"I wanted to share with you Aaron's list of supplies he's requested." She flung the first sheet at him.

Aaron simply nodded in agreement, as if to say, "Yes, that's my list, and it's completely practical. I'm sure you'll agree."

Her *dat* adjusted his wire-rim glasses and leaned back in his chair. After reading for a moment, he glanced up at Aaron. "*Gut* list. I should have thought of the chainsaw. Fallen limbs are a hazard to guests, for sure and certain. Excellent job, Aaron. I'll pass this on to Gideon. He should have what you need by midweek."

Drats. This meeting wasn't starting on the right note. And worse than that, Aaron was now grinning like the notorious Cheshire cat.

Amos reached for his coffee and took an appreciative sip before returning his attention to Bethany. "Plainly, you have something else to say."

"I do." Bethany sat up straighter and reminded herself that she had been the manager of the RV park for the last five months. She knew what her guests needed and wanted. Certainly she knew those things better than Aaron, who had been there for less than six hours.

She pushed the second sheet of paper toward her father.

"Plain and Simple Resort, huh? That has a nice ring to it."

Bethany didn't dare look at Aaron. She could feel him smiling. She needed to stand up for herself, for her vision. She needed to do so this very minute, or there might not be another chance.

"*Dat*, don't you see that a resort is not what we provide here? We provide a plain and simple camping experience. That's why *Englischers* come here—to experience the plain life. They don't need a firepit or a dog park or a gazebo." She was getting hot all over again.

Forcing her voice down, she added, "Perhaps you can explain our image to Aaron, as he's unwilling or unable to listen to me, though I am, technically, the manager of the RV park."

Amos removed his glasses, pulled a cotton rag from his desk drawer and methodically cleaned the lenses. After he'd returned the rag and donned the glasses, he finally looked directly at Bethany and then shifted his gaze to Aaron.

"Since you're here, I suppose that you would like to add something to this conversation."

"*Ya*, for sure and certain I would. I learned a lot about RV people while working in Sarasota the past seven years. It's true, what Bethany says, that they want a taste of the plain and simple life."

"But?"

"But my experience is that they want that taste with the same luxuries and accommodations that they're used to."

"Give me an example."

"Okay." Aaron sat up straighter, his fingertips tapping a beat against the arm of the chair. "Pets."

"That's your example?" Bethany bit back any additional commentary when her *dat* tossed her *the look*.

"*Englischers* enjoy seeing our buggy horses as well as our work horses. Perhaps it reminds them of how their grandparents used to farm. But they wouldn't give up their trucks or motor homes in order to travel by horse and buggy."

Bethany couldn't resist "No one is talking about their vehicles."

Aaron kept his attention focused on Amos. "Instead, they connect to animals by having pets. I would guess eighty percent of RV people have pets—lots of dogs, a few cats, even birds occasionally. The dog park wouldn't cost much—a small fence, perhaps a bench, a holder for dog pickup bags and a trash can."

Amos was nodding before Aaron finished talking, and Bethany knew she'd lost that particular point. "Seems like a *gut* idea to me. What's the downside, Bethany?"

"The downside is the entire image that we're trying to project. We don't want to be a resort."

Aaron remained irritatingly silent, as if his list of ideas spoke for itself.

"Our image is important," Amos conceded. "But that image won't matter unless we stay in business."

"Of course, we'll stay in business. What do you even mean by that?"

"I mean…" Now her *dat* sat up straighter and glanced at his stack of paper.

Bethany could sense the window closing on their meeting.

"Each portion of this market must operate at a profit. The RV park has been open for five months now, but it still isn't running at a profit. I'm willing to invest a moderate amount of funds and give you both a little more time, but soon your portion of this business needs to be profitable. Aaron, your list seems like a *gut* start."

"Back up a minute, please." A cold dread had seized Bethany's heart. "What exactly are you saying? We have to show a profit—even though you've doubled our employee cost—or…or what?"

"I'm saying that if you don't start running a profit soon, certainly by the end of the summer, then we'll have to close the RV park down."

"Close it down?" Bethany popped out of her chair. "You can't mean that."

"I do. Remember the time we tried to have a merry-go-round and pony rides? Sounded like a great idea, but the cost was higher than the proceeds. We had to close that down. In fact, if I remember right it was in the same area where the RV park is now. A market is a living, breathing thing, and it changes over time, or it should. Never forget, though, that it is first and foremost a business."

He pulled the stack of paper toward him, and Aaron stood to go. But Bethany couldn't just walk away. She couldn't leave things like this. She needed Aaron to know that she was in charge and that her vision was the one they would pursue.

"We can't be profitable until we decide what we're going to be. We need a roadmap. If Aaron is pulling us toward his resort, and I'm trying to make us appear more plain...well, how is that supposed to work?"

Her *dat* peered over his glasses. "Tell you what. Aaron, pick three things on your list that you'd like to do first, order the supplies through Gideon, and then implement them over the next six weeks. Bethany, you keep doing your thing of emphasizing the plain and simple angle. In six weeks, we'll meet again and weigh the two...see whose vision has had the best response."

"Sounds fair to me." Aaron was grinning at her as he said it, provoking her just as he had when they were back in school.

It made Bethany want to stamp her foot. "Fine. But would you please tell him that for the next six weeks, I'm the one in charge of the RV park? We can't have two bosses."

"Actually, I think in this case we can. You'll be co-managers for now." Amos picked up a pen, officially ending the meeting.

Bethany felt as if steam must be shooting out of her ears.

They were nearly out the front door of the office building when Aaron tugged on her arm. "Want to get some lunch?" He nodded in the direction of the market's diner.

She was about to say no when her stomach betrayed her, growling long and loud.

"Come on. We can talk about how we're going to stay out of each other's way for the next six weeks."

Which was the only reason that she agreed to spend another half hour with him. The last thing she wanted to do was eat lunch with Aaron King, but she was hungry. Maybe while he was eating, she could find a way to subvert his plan.

Aaron could tell that Bethany was miffed, and he knew he had a better chance of being successful if she was on his side. The one thing he didn't know, couldn't fathom at all, was how to win her over.

He'd ordered a roast beef sandwich with fries. She'd opted for the chicken and dumplings. She had attacked the food with gusto for her first three bites, then dropped her spoon, staring off across the diner and shaking her head.

"Things aren't that bad, are they?" He tried to make it sound like a joke.

Bethany slowly pulled her gaze back to him. "It's not good."

She took another bite of the dumplings, staring at his fries as she did so.

"Want some?"

She shook her head no, but something in her eyes said yes. He pushed the plate toward her. Begrudgingly, she ate one and then another. A smile tried to tug free from the corners of her mouth.

"Comfort food. Right?" He snagged his sandwich but left the plate of fries sitting between them.

"I suppose."

"Why do you dislike me so much, Bethany?"

"Do you want a list?"

He laughed. "At least we're being honest now."

She squirted ketchup onto his plate, then picked up the salt and pepper shakers and wiggled them, raising her eyebrows in question.

"Sure."

She vigorously salted and peppered the fries, ate two more, then sat back. "Why did you come back to Shipshe?"

"Why not?"

"That isn't an answer. If Sarasota was so great, why come back to your old hometown?"

He wasn't about to share the details of his family's problems with anyone, least of all someone he would be seeing every day. He didn't need the looks of pity or the concerned questions. Instead, he sidestepped the question. "Seemed like a *gut* idea."

He finished his sandwich, ate a few more of the fries, then stood to refill his soda.

When he returned, she was still sulking, but she had a bit more feistiness in her eyes. He didn't know whether he should be relieved or worried.

"I didn't realize we weren't making a profit," she finally admitted.

"Sometimes that can be solved by raising the prices, but I don't think your *dat* will want to do that."

"*Nein*. He won't."

"The other solution is that you need more people in your park."

She shook her head as if she didn't understand what he was saying.

"Think of it as a yarn shop."

Now Bethany stared at him pointedly, cocking her head and waiting. Aaron nearly laughed.

Bethany struck him as two different people. The one sitting before him now did not mind admitting that she had no idea what he was talking about. The one that had been confronting her *dat* had been more like a strong winter wind. How could someone so slight be such a force to reckon with? Maybe it was true what they said, that the biggest surprises came in the smallest packages.

"Just…let me finish." Aaron picked up the salt shaker and set it between them, then the pepper shaker and bottle of ketchup. "Pretend these are bundles of yarn."

"Skeins?"

"Whatever. Now consider how many of these *skeins* of yarn a shop needs to sell to cover their costs—electricity, rental of the space, employees, plus the base cost of the product."

"Probably a lot. After all that, I doubt they make fifty cents a skein." A frown had formed between her eyes.

She looked adorable when she focused on a thing.

"Now, they can raise their prices, but that doesn't help much because some people will stop shopping there."

"I probably would, especially if I could find the yarn cheaper somewhere else."

"Exactly, which is why raising the price of a thing often won't solve the problem. On the other hand, if they attract more people to their shop, then they can cover their expenses more easily. Customers are happy because the prices are reasonable—they tell their friends, which brings even more customers."

"How do they keep those new customers?"

"Great question. Maybe they offer yarn classes."

"Knitting or crochet."

"I guess. Or they could offer other items for sale…"

"Like craft books or handmade items that have an 'Amish made' sign on them." She sat back now, thinking. Finally she asked, "Is that how you did it in Sarasota? How you made your *resort* so profitable?"

It was Aaron's turn to stare across the room. He missed Sarasota Bay, the gulf, the fishing and swimming. He missed feeling like he was making the important decisions of his life. Instead of being where he wanted to be, he was back here, cleaning up his *dat*'s mess.

Those problems weren't Bethany's fault though, and if things went well, if he could get her on his side, he'd make enough money to get his *mamm* out of the hole his *dat* had dug. Then maybe he could return to his life in Florida.

He didn't share any of that though. The less she knew about his personal problems, the better. He didn't need her feeling sorry for him. "Sarasota is a tourist location…"

"So is Shipshe."

"True, but I'd guess there are more campers in Florida year-round than in Northern Indiana. Camping in the snow can be rather tedious. Being stuck indoors when you're indoors is small—well, that isn't much fun."

"Fair point." She moved the salt and pepper shakers back to the side of the table. "So what do we do?"

"If we work together, get our number of guests up, persuade people to stay longer and to return regularly…" He shrugged and drank the last of his coke. "The RV park will be fine. We won't have to raise your prices, and our jobs will be secure—at least until you marry and don't want it anymore."

She drew back, frowning at him.

"What? What did I say?"

She pushed the plate of now cold fries back toward him. "You think you know me, Aaron King, but you don't."

"I never claimed that I did."

"What is it the *Englisch* say? Stay in your lane."

"My lane?"

She was standing now, waving her hands around to make some point he was not catching, the look of defiance again firmly in place. "Stay on your side of the office. Whatever. Focus on your resort ideas, but in six weeks' time, my *dat* will see that my ideas are better."

"Oh, you think so?"

"I do, and then you'll be busted down to assistant manager."

"What is your problem?" Now he was irritated. He did not understand women. In particular, he did not understand the beautiful one standing in front of him and waving her arms.

"You. My problem is you." And with that, she turned and strode out of the room.

The only person left in the dining hall to witness their argument was the young girl working behind the register. She looked to be fifteen, probably just out of school. Rather than pretending she didn't see the argument, she shrugged her shoulders, then returned her attention to cleaning the counters.

He could have headed back to the RV park, but he didn't. Aaron borrowed a sheet of paper and pen from the girl at the register. Her name was Tabitha, and she was able to tell him where to find Gideon.

So, he'd gone back to the table, pushed their dishes out of the way and made his list of supplies for three of the projects—the three that he thought would make the biggest difference and cost the least. Then he went in search of Gideon.

He found him in the auction barn.

"You're the new guy—in the RV park."

"I am."

Gideon looked to be the same height and weight as Aaron, but something about his expression indicated he was older. He looked so relaxed. He held a clipboard, had a pencil stuck behind his ear and was surrounded by at least thirty boxes.

"Did I catch you at a bad time?"

"Not at all. What can I do for you?"

Aaron handed over the sheet of paper, explained what he was doing and that Amos had approved the projects.

"Sounds *gut* to me."

They talked through the supply list, and Gideon made a couple of suggestions that would lower the costs. After twenty minutes, it was all settled, and they walked out of the auction barn and stood in the weak sunshine that had finally pierced the clouds.

"How are things going with Bethany?"

"Not that great, to be honest."

Instead of being surprised, Gideon grinned and clapped him on the shoulder. "The Yoder girls are a stubborn lot, but once you get to know them, you'll find…well, you'll find that they're worth getting to know."

Aaron practically slapped his forehead. He'd completely forgotten that Gideon was about to marry Bethany's *schweschder*. "You're marrying the older girl."

"One week from today. Becca is older than Bethany by a few years—five or six."

"I didn't mean any disrespect."

"Don't apologize. I was at a complete loss when I started working here, and I was competing with Becca for my job. Not so different from your situation."

"That's a story I'd like to hear, though I can't imagine mine ending as well as yours. It certainly isn't going to end in marriage."

"Never say never."

Which made Aaron laugh, because the idea of Bethany being interested in him romantically was as farfetched as the idea of him taking a buggy to the moon.

"I'll get these things ordered tomorrow morning."

"Danki."

"And if you ever need to talk, just come and find me."

Aaron knew he wouldn't do that, but he thanked Gideon and walked back toward the RV park. He'd never really had a friend that he talked to in the way that Gideon was suggesting. It had always been too awkward. Friends visited your home. Friends knew the truth about your parents. He'd avoided both of those things at all costs.

In this case, the cost of having a bipolar *dat* and enabling *mamm* was one more friendship that would never develop.

Aaron told himself he didn't care. Everything was going to be okay. He had his *bruder*. He and Ethan stood by each other, and though he sometimes felt lonely, he reminded himself that he wasn't here forever. Six months maybe—a year at the most. Then he'd be back in Sarasota, where he didn't have to hide the details of his family life because there was no chance of anyone stumbling upon the truth.

Chapter Five

Unfortunately, Bethany didn't have much time over the next week to focus on her irritation with Aaron. Her *schweschder*'s wedding was fast approaching. Becca would be the first of the Yoder girls to marry. It was shaping up to be quite the event. The wedding was scheduled to take place the following Tuesday.

Bethany spent every spare moment of the week before finishing up her wedding gift. She'd known from the day that Becca and Gideon had announced their intention to marry, way back in December, that she wanted to give them a double wedding ring quilt. She'd worked diligently on it, and everything was done but the binding. Still, hand-binding a queen-sized quilt was no laughing matter. First, she had to cut the fabric, then iron the long strips, which she did at work since she had an electric iron there. Next, she needed to sew it onto the four sides of the quilt, press it over and sew the back side.

She was working on that, on the back side, the day before the wedding. She'd stayed home from work, though it bothered her terribly to know that Aaron was in their office without her, probably plotting her demise.

Ada was giving the living room one last touch-up, though they'd cleaned the house thoroughly on Saturday. She wore an older pale yellow dress and flitted about the room straightening rugs and lamps and books as she dusted. Ada reminded Bethany of a spring flower—fresh and sunny and full of life.

"I'm glad that I'm not the one tying the bow."

"You mean tying the knot." Eunice walked in carrying an armful of carnations that she'd picked up from the local florist. Traditionally, Amish put celery sticks into glasses and used them as centerpieces for the long tables of wedding guests.

Becca was not much for tradition. "White carnations—that's what I'd love to have."

Their *dat* had kissed her on the top of the head and murmured, "Then you shall have carnations." He was getting soft in his old age, or perhaps he was simply thrilled that one of his five *doschdern* was finally marrying.

"I don't want to tie anything," Ada admitted. "I'm lucky *dat* is allowing me to take two days off from my school duties."

The previous fall, Ada had thought being a teacher's apprentice would be the best job in Shipshewana, then throughout the winter, she'd looked for any acceptable reason to quit. Her *dat* had told her in no uncertain terms that she would honor her commitment for the entire year. Now that it was April, she was looking forward to her freedom.

Sarah walked in with two pairs of scissors, passed one to Eunice and plopped down on the couch. "Let's make flower arrangements."

As Bethany sewed and Ada dusted, Sarah and Eunice cut flower stems—plopping them into mason jars. The room was immediately filled with the heady fragrance of the flowers. For Bethany, they brought to mind cloves and cinnamon, though she couldn't have said why...some long forgotten memory, she supposed. Had their mother loved carnations?

Of course, they discussed the wedding as they worked.

"Where is Becca?" Eunice brushed the cut stems into a bucket. She would toss them into the compost pile when they were finished. Any excuse to be outside or in the barn was quickly snatched up by Eunice.

"Gideon's family arrived from Texas last night. She's over at Nathan's making sure they are settled in and have everything they need."

"Nathan's going to miss Gideon." Bethany turned the quilt and continued sewing binding on the second side.

"He won't have a chance." Sarah snipped another carnation stem.."Haven't you heard? Gideon's youngest *bruder* has decided to stay."

"I hadn't heard that," Bethany admitted. "I suppose I've been pretty distracted by Aaron King trying to steal my job."

"Let him have it, Beth." Ada flopped down on the floor next to the chair where Bethany was sitting. "You can take off the summer and pal around with me."

"That sounds great, but I like my job, thank you very much."

"And I doubt *dat* will allow you to pal around all summer." Eunice shrugged when Ada glowered at her. "You know how he is. Everyone should be a productive member of the community. Now, if you were engaged to marry..."

"Ack. Never mind. Give me another job."

"What do you have against marriage, Ada?" Bethany paused mid-stitch. She'd always thought that Ada was the prettiest of them. Plus she was pleasant to be around. She could probably snag any eligible bachelor in their community.

"Let's see." Ada put her hands on the floor behind her and craned her neck back to stare at the ceiling. "I wouldn't get to go to singings anymore. I'd probably have my own house, so there would be loads of cooking and cleaning. And then the babies would start."

"You make it sound terrible." Sarah tossed Ada a reproving look as she began to set the flower-filled glass jars into a box lid. "Marriage is a blessing."

"You're one to talk." Ada laughed. "I've had at least three people ask me if Bethany is going to be a runaway bride like you."

Sarah shrugged off the insult. Bethany knew that Sarah had heard such comments plenty of times before, and she'd long ago stopped explaining to anyone why she'd ducked out of not one but two engagements. She had her reasons, and that was good enough for her. Bethany wished she had that sort of confidence and clarity about things. She wished she was more like her eldest *schweschder*.

"I'm not getting harnessed until I'm older." Ada leaned closer to Bethany.

"Hitched." Eunice grinned as she corrected her. "You're not getting *hitched* until you're older."

Ada tossed her *kapp* strings over her shoulders and turned her attention to Bethany. "Beautiful quilt, Beth. Becca and Gideon are going to love it."

They were interrupted by the sound of buggy wheels.

"I best get out there and help with Peanut." Eunice was no doubt looking for an excuse to be freed from more wedding preparations. She had a mechanical side to her brain that meant she was always happier when she was out of the house—whether it be unharnessing a horse or building a new contraption.

Hearing Becca's voice on the front porch, Bethany swept up the quilt and binding and fled to her room. She knew it was silly, but she didn't want Becca seeing her gift until the wedding. She wanted it to be a surprise.

She sat in her room, sewing and listening to the sounds of her family below—her *schweschdern* laughing, Gideon's voice interrupting here and there. It was odd to hear a man's voice in the house, but she supposed she would get used to it. Gideon and Becca would be living with them, at least for the first year. Bethany had always shared a room with Ada, but now Sarah was moving in with Eunice so that Gideon and Becca could have the largest of the upstairs bedrooms.

She finished binding the quilt, carefully folded it, then ran her fingertips over the interlocking rings. Since they were Amish, they didn't wear jewelry of any kind—not even wedding rings. But the symbolism remained strong of two rings intertwined—forever a part of one another, lives irrevocably woven into a single sacred unit.

Bethany had no idea what that would feel like. She honestly could not imagine it. Sure, she knew lots of people who were married. Though she was only twenty, most of her schoolmates had already wed. But she hadn't viewed a marriage up close. She'd been two years old when their *mamm* had died from uterine cancer. Both sets of grandparents had passed as well. She'd not spent much time around married couples.

And in the deepest parts of her heart, she didn't think she'd ever know what being united with someone felt like. She didn't believe there was anyone out there for her—a perfect match, one true love, her soul mate. She'd heard all those terms tossed around, but she'd never felt anything even remotely resembling love. Occasionally, it made her sad to think of remaining single all of her life—the years stretching out like a road, one she would walk alone.

Her *schweschdern* would probably, one by one, marry off.

Would she stay in the family home taking care of her *dat* when he was a *grossdaddi*?

That thought nearly made her laugh. It was hard to picture her *dat* as old, unable to work, sitting in a rocker on the front porch. Even his heart attack the year before hadn't slowed him down for long, and now—due to the doctor's orders and Sarah's careful cooking—he'd lost twenty pounds.

She supposed it was natural to have such melancholy thoughts since change was, literally, in the air. The thing was, she couldn't imagine any change for her.

Then Aaron King's face popped in her mind, but she pushed it away. Whoever married Aaron King—with his *Englisch* ideas and maddening work ethic—would have their hands full. Perhaps she should start praying for the poor woman now.

Aaron was not happy about wasting an entire day at Becca Yoder's wedding. "I barely know her," he complained as he reached for his Sunday hat.

"You work with her *schweschder*." Ethan purposely bumped his shoulder against Aaron's. "And you know Gideon. You told me you work with him."

"*Ya*. He's the assistant manager of the entire market, and he'd probably rather have me at work getting things done."

"I think you're simply being competitive, wanting to finish all of your new projects while Bethany is distracted with the wedding."

There was no use denying that, so Aaron didn't try.

Their *mamm* joined them on the porch. She had her best clothes on. The dress and *kapp* were clean and pressed, but they had seen better days. All of their clothes were in need of replacement, but when he was at home or work, Aaron didn't think about it. Seeing his small family together dressed for a wedding brought home once again just how poor they were.

His *mamm*'s purse strap was over her shoulder, and she was carrying her wedding gift—two hot pads that she'd pieced together from scraps of fabric. She smiled at her sons. "Perfect weather for a wedding, *ya*?"

And then she walked down the porch steps toward the waiting buggy.

Ethan grinned at him. "You're not getting out of this one, *bruder*. Might as well smile and enjoy it."

It was a relatively short drive to the Yoders, but Aaron still managed to use the time to sink deeper into his discontent. He had been to many weddings in his life. When someone in your church married, everyone attended. Each family brought a gift that could be used by the new couple—no matter how small. Everyone joined in celebrating the new life for the bride and groom. It was an all-day affair with preaching beginning at ten in the morning, followed by singing, and then finally the exchange of vows. After that was lunch, games for everyone under twenty-five or so, and then an evening meal. Aaron sincerely hoped he didn't have to stay that long.

He'd been to the Yoder house when he was younger. He'd been to every house in their congregation. Church services were rotated through the members' homes. Somehow, his *mamm* had always avoided hosting the service at their place. He supposed that was because the bishop was aware of their situation. It was just another way that Aaron and his family were different.

As they approached the Yoder drive, Aaron felt as if he were stepping into a different world. Well-tended pastures, good fencing, a nice-sized barn and a two-story house that could have been on the cover of the *Shipshewana Visitors Magazine*. The house looked as if it had recently received a fresh coat of white paint. Dark green shutters hung to the sides of the large windows, and the wraparound porch sported rocking chairs, bright colored pillows and lush green plants.

The Yoders seemed to have it all.

Of course, the weather was perfect, even slightly warm for an April day.

"Don't look so glum, *bruder*. Our place will look like this soon."

"Do you mean after we repair the barn, put up new fencing, plant a garden and renovate the house?"

His *mamm*'s voice was gentle, which somehow made what she had to say all the more stinging. "You cannot do everything at once, but you can do something at once."

A proverb! She thought a proverb was the answer to

their situation. He honestly believed she could not grasp the seriousness of their financial difficulties. She would be homeless if their plan didn't work. They all would be.

Aaron was sitting in the back seat of the buggy, and he was glad for that. He preferred to be alone with his foul mood. He didn't want to have a terrible attitude, but he didn't understand why some people had so much and others so little. Why was Bethany Yoder born into the perfect family with a solid income and many hands to do the work?

Why was he born into a family of two *bruders* with a *dat* who seemed to actively work against them and a *mamm* who seemed incapable of standing up to her husband?

Ethan directed their mare, Misty, toward the front circular drive. Good grief—the Yoders even had a family dog that looked freshly bathed and was sporting a white carnation tucked into his dog collar. Aaron plastered on a smile as he helped his *mamm* out of the buggy. Ethan drove over to a teenager who was parking buggies and unharnessing the horses, releasing them into an adjacent pasture.

They walked around to the back of the house, and Aaron blinked his eyes in surprise. He'd thought the front of the house looked like the cover of a magazine, but he had nothing to compare the back of the house to…maybe an *Englisch* movie set?

The yard had been freshly mowed and the seating for guests arranged in a semicircular fashion. The happy couple would exchange their vows beneath an arch that had been decorated with carnations. The flowers seemed to be everywhere. Long rows of tables had been positioned to the right. Each table was covered with a

white table cloth and decorated with mason jars filled
with even more carnations.

How many flowers had they bought?

How much had that cost?

As Aaron walked his *mamm* to a place where they
could sit, he looked around in disbelief. He'd guessed
the Yoders were wealthy, but he hadn't expected this.
Oh, he'd known that the wedding would be well attended—not only by their congregation but also by local
merchants who worked alongside Amos. Truthfully, he'd
never seen a wedding this large. The rows of church
pews were only the beginning of it. In addition, Amos
had apparently rented out chairs that had been set up
in a fan-shaped wedge away from where the bishop
stood even now.

They'd arrived just in time.

Aaron gritted his teeth, determined to escape as soon
as possible. He barely listened to the sermons, and he
certainly didn't join in the singing. But he couldn't
stop himself from paying attention when Gideon and
Becca stepped forward to say their vows. Becca wore
a new pastel blue dress. Aaron could see that it was
simply made, something that she could use for a Sunday dress—still, it was new, unlike his *mamm*'s dress.
Gideon, too, was wearing his Sunday best.

It wasn't only their clothing that captured Aaron's attention. Gideon and Becca both wore looks of complete
devotion on their faces as they held hands and waited
for Bishop Ezekiel to begin the sharing of vows. Ezekiel
was in his eighties, with a white beard and a bum knee
that required him to use a cane. He paused before speaking, studying the crowd of people gathered to celebrate

with the couple. Finally, Ezekiel smiled and turned his attention to the two standing directly in front of him.

Combing his fingers through his beard, he smiled. "Big day, *ya*?"

Everyone laughed. Gideon and Becca nodded, and any tension in the gathering seemed to dissipate on the light spring breeze. It was then he noticed Bethany and her *schweschdern* sitting on the front bench—the four remaining girls sitting shoulder to shoulder with their *dat* at the end.

Ezekiel's voice was still strong, easy to listen to, and filled with wisdom and kindness if a voice could carry such things. "Do you, Gideon Fisher, and you, Rebecca Yoder, vow to remain together until death?"

"We do." Their voices were soft but certain. They were speaking to one another, oblivious now to the crowd of witnesses.

"And will you both be loyal to one another?"

"We will."

"Will you care for one another during adversity?"

"We will."

"During affliction?"

"Yes." Their responses sealed their commitment to one another, but the words weren't necessary. Their expressions told the entire story—what they felt for one another.

Aaron tried to imagine what that would feel like and failed.

"During sickness?"

"We will."

Ezekiel's smile broadened. He placed his hands over theirs, but he addressed the guests, the friends, the family. "It is my great honor to inform you both that everyone here—your friends and family in Christ, and I, as your bishop—wishes you the blessing and the mercy of God."

And it was at that moment that Aaron felt a sharp pain in his chest. It was deeper than envy or resentment. Far more agonizing than either of those things. When he saw Gideon and Becca turn toward the crowd, when he noticed the large group of family at the front—family representing both the bride and the groom, he understood that this was something he would never have.

He'd never have a large family to support him.

He and Ethan might be able to work hard enough to have a well-tended farm, though not one as prosperous as the Yoders'.

But they couldn't create a family that would stand with them, support them, celebrate with them.

Nein. It would always be him and Ethan standing together against the harshness of the world, and lurking behind them, casting his shadow on everything they did, would be their *dat.* It was a legacy that he couldn't outrun.

Ezekiel now smiled broadly. "Go forth in the Lord's name. You are now man and wife."

Ninety minutes later, they'd eaten the midday meal. Aaron's *mamm* seemed content to sit and visit with the other women, and he couldn't deny her that, though he was more than ready to leave. Ethan was standing at the pasture fence, talking with a group of men—no doubt about crops and weather and which animals brought in the highest profit.

Aaron stood, walked to the corner table and congratulated Gideon and Becca. Both thanked him warmly. They were nice people. He knew that. It wasn't their fault that their life was idyllic and his wasn't.

Unable to sit still any longer, he walked around the perimeter of those gathered, then circled back and found himself standing by the gift table, staring at the bounty stacked there. The table was literally overflowing with presents—dishes, linens, silverware, everything a couple would need to set up house. Some gifts were elaborate and had probably taken months to make—like the quilt folded and placed near the back of the table. Then there was his mother's paltry offering of two hot pads placed in front of the quilt and next to an iron skillet.

"*Englischers* wrap their gifts. Can you imagine?"

He tried not to jerk at the sound of Bethany's voice, pretended to be appreciating the wedding gifts.

She shook her head as if the foolishness of wrapping presents was beyond her imagination. "I like it this way. Gideon and Becca can see all the well wishes in the gifts, maybe even peek into their future when they'll need mixing bowls and coffee pots."

She reached forward and ran her fingertips across a quilt.

"Did you make that for them?"

"I did." She glanced at him, smiled awkwardly, then turned her attention back to the quilt. "It's what I'm best at—quilting, knitting, embroidery."

"How did you end up working at the RV park?"

Bethany laughed and shook her head as if she couldn't imagine how that had happened.

He glanced to his left then and saw the trailer with the words—*Louise's Wedding Caterer*. He was aware that many people used a caterer. Many weddings like this one had over five hundred people present, and all were fed lunch. Those who stayed through the day were fed dinner. The caterer not only provided the food but also supplied the dishes for the entire event.

Aaron understood that this wasn't a Sunday potluck. But still, he couldn't stop the surge of jealousy, the resentment rising in him at the sight of the catering truck. It was, literally, the last straw. Perhaps because he hadn't been able to talk to anyone about his feelings, Bethany became the target of his words. "I see that your *dat* ordered the wedding caterer."

"*Ya*. I can't imagine trying to cook for this many ourselves."

"Well, I'm sure it's money he will never miss."

"What's that supposed to mean?"

"It means that Gideon and Becca don't need these gifts because they'll never want for anything. Your family is among the wealthiest in our district. Your life—it's…" He knew he should stop then, but he was on a roll. Stopping would have required restraint and wisdom, and he did not have either of those at the moment.

He turned to face her, his arms crossed and his words weighted with accusation. "Your life is like a dream. You don't even need your job at the RV park. It's just something to keep you entertained—no more."

"I can't believe you're saying these things to me, Aaron King. What right do you have to—"

"I have every right, because I have to witness your abundance while my *mamm* worked for weeks on two small hot pads that Becca will probably put into the charity box."

"She would never do that."

Instead of his words upsetting her, they'd apparently unleashed her growing irritation with him. Bethany's face colored, and she clenched her hands at her side. It reminded him of when they were young scholars. Even then, there had been a marked difference between their lives. No wonder he'd teased her so. She had always had everything that he didn't.

But he'd been out of line to say so, especially on her *schweschder*'s wedding day. He understood that, and so he didn't back away from her anger.

He deserved whatever was coming.

She stepped closer—too close. He could smell the lilac shampoo she'd used, see the freckles scattered across the bridge of her nose. He'd never stood this close to her, not even at the RV park. They'd been careful to keep a good distance apart. Now the tips of her toes were practically touching his.

"You don't know anything about us, Aaron King. You think that we have a perfect life? A fairy-tale life? You have a *mamm* and *dat*, if I remember correctly. I never even knew my *mamm*. I can't even remember what she looked like or the sound of her voice."

Tears filled her eyes, and he felt the first inkling of remorse wash over him.

"My *dat* has had to do the work here as well as at the market for nearly all his life." She shook her head in disgust and stepped back, turned away, then reversed course like a storm that wasn't quite done with him yet. "If we have more than others, then we give more than others as well. Becca has devoted herself to MDS missions, and Gideon is now supporting his *bruder* here because their community in Beeville offers very few opportunities. You don't know them, and you don't know me."

She raised her chin and crossed her arms, daring him to contradict her. "And do you know why you don't know anyone else? It's because you've never taken the time. You're much too busy thinking about yourself."

And then she was gone, leaving him standing there by the gift table staring at a double wedding ring quilt and two potholders sitting side by side but, in fact, worlds apart.

Chapter Six

The weather turned bleak the next day and stayed that way through the rest of the week. It was cold, rainy, gloomy. Basically, a perfect reflection of Aaron's mood. Bethany had avoided him every day at the RV park. He'd finally resorted to working in the supply shed rather than endure her silence. It had been a long week, and by Friday he'd rather have gone to bed early—without dinner and without speaking with Ethan or his *mamm*.

But he wasn't that selfish.

Although much of what Bethany had said had been true, he didn't think only of himself. He also thought of his *bruder* and his *mamm*.

So here he was in the barn, helping with the evening chores.

They had mucked out Misty's stall, and Aaron was now oiling the harness so that it wouldn't rub sore spots on the old mare. Ethan had been cleaning his farming tools. Ethan kept a neat barn. He was determined to make what few things they had last as long as possible.

Aaron's mood had grown as dark as the weather,

though he could barely think over the sound of rain pounding against the roof.

"What's bothering you, *bruder*?"

Aaron pointed at the rain, dripping steadily through the hole in the barn's roof and splattering into a bucket. "That. That's bothering me, among other things."

"I'm aware there are holes in the barn's roof."

"And the house."

"There too, but you've been in a foul mood since Tuesday, so I don't think it's caused by the rain."

Aaron shrugged, then, because he couldn't think of any reason not to, he confessed the details of his argument with Bethany. "Needless to say, we avoided each other the rest of the week at the market."

"Huh."

"That's it. That's all you have to say? Huh?"

"I don't suppose you need me to point out she's right."

"How do you figure that?" Aaron walked over to the door to Misty's stall and stopped to scratch the old gray mare between the eyes. She nodded her head in appreciation. Mares were like that—easy to understand, easy to make happy.

"You really want me to list all the ways you're wrong?"

"Sure. I can think of nothing I'd rather hear."

Instead of being offended by Aaron's sarcastic tone, Ethan leaned against the wall of the opposite stall—an empty stall because his family had never been able to afford a second horse—and crossed his arms. "While it's true that the Yoder family is doing well, it wasn't always so. In the beginning, Amos was simply an auctioneer at the market."

"How do you know that?"

"Ezekiel told me the story once when I was younger, when I was still comparing my life to others." Ethan stretched his neck to the right, then the left and finally back. He stared up at the ceiling. "Amos was a young widower with five *doschdern*. He was trying to run his farm and also took a job at the market because he needed the extra money."

Now he looked directly at Aaron. "Not so different from our story."

"Very different, in my opinion."

Ethan shrugged. "Regardless, he worked his way up in the market until he became the general manager. As for his *doschdern*, word is that he's worried what will happen to them if he dies."

"Is he ill?"

"*Nein*, I don't think so. He had an episode with his heart less than a year ago, but he seems fully recovered. Still, none of us knows the number of our days, and they have no extended family. Both sets of grandparents have passed. I supposed he'd like to see each of his *doschdern* settled with a husband."

"So why haven't they married? They're all old enough."

"True." Now Ethan was smiling. "I've heard some people are stubborn about such things."

"Don't look at me." Aaron held up his hands, palms out. "I'm in no position to marry."

"I suppose neither of us are—not now. But one day we will be, *bruder*. One day we will be."

Neither spoke for a moment. The rain continued to drum against the roof, the drops continued to fall into the bucket. Finally, Aaron admitted, "I shouldn't have said what I did to Bethany. I feel bad about it. Tuesday was a special day for her family, and I let my bitterness spill over and stain it."

"Something easily fixed by an apology."

"What apology has ever been easy?"

Ethan laughed. "You have me there."

They put the barn to rights, closed it up tight against the weather and stood outside under the eave studying their house.

Aaron wrestled with what he wanted to ask. What was the point? He didn't expect an answer that would help, but then again…bottling it up inside didn't seem to be working for him either. "Don't you ever feel… angry? Doesn't the unfairness of it bother you?"

"Anger takes a lot of energy, Aaron. Energy I need to save for the fields. As for the unfairness, well, who ever said life was fair? I don't remember it being in the Good Book. I don't remember any such promise."

"When did you become such a wise old man?"

"Wise? A few years ago, I believe." He rubbed a hand across his clean-shaven face. "*Ya*, I believe it was three years ago while I was plowing a field in Sugar Creek. Suddenly wisdom descended from the clouds—"

Aaron reached out and pushed him.

Ethan laughed. "But old, that I will not claim to be. There's still time for us, Aaron. Still time to make up for the mistakes of our parents. Still time to start fresh."

Oh, how Aaron wished he believe that.

The problem was that deep in the most secret parts of his heart, he didn't.

"I can't stand the thought of him coming home next week."

"We knew from the beginning it was a temporary stay."

Aaron's stomach felt as if it was grappling with sour milk. He forced a deep breath, tried not to give in to the feelings of despair. "It's too soon though. He can't possibly be…well."

"He can be better, and perhaps that will be enough."

And then Ethan did something that Aaron didn't expect. He and his *bruder* had never been physically demonstrative—no one in their family was. It was as if they were afraid to get too close to one another.

But Ethan reached out, put his hand on Aaron's shoulder, squeezed, then smiled. "The bishop is on our side. *Mamm* is on our side. We all want *Dat* to get well, but we won't let him do the things he's done before."

"How will we stop him?" The question felt as if it came from the depth of his soul, certainly from the worst of his nightmares.

"We're men now, Aaron. We're no longer boys. Somehow, we will take care of our *mamm*, and we'll take care of our *dat* if he allows us to."

What was left unsaid was the other possibility.

What if Zackary King didn't allow them to take care of him? What if he insisted on going his own way, as he had every time before? What if he took the sum of the work that they'd done over the last few weeks and uprooted it all?

Ethan nodded toward the house. "We best be getting in. It's late."

Aaron shook his head. "In a minute."

Despite his *bruder*'s words, the old worries churned in his stomach. He wasn't ready to face his *mamm*, to pretend that everything was fine, because he had a strong suspicion born of years of experience that everything was about to get much worse.

By the time Aaron left the market on Tuesday, Bethany was ready to scream. She'd never been good at handling conflict. It was one reason that she preferred yarn work, needlework, anything that didn't involve people.

Aaron had been out of line when he'd spoken to her at the wedding. Since then, he'd gone from sulky to silent to morose. She dreaded being in the same room with him. A dark cloud seemed to follow him around like a loyal pet.

Her *dat* had hired a driver to take him to Middlebury on business, so Bethany had to ride home alone—allowing her to sink into even deeper despair. By the time she arrived at the house, a headache was forming at the base of her neck.

"Goodness, Sis. You don't look so *gut*." Eunice met her outside the barn. "Long day?"

"It was, and by the way, you have grease on your forehead."

"I'm not surprised. Working on a solar-powered feeder. Gideon and *Dat* are talking about buying more animals, though they hadn't decided on what before the wedding. Still, I'd like to have the feeders working by the time the purchase is made. It'll mean less work for everyone."

Bethany was hoping for goats or maybe sheep. Either were adorable and would definitely raise her spirits, but that purchase was at least a month off.

"I'll take care of Oreo in just a minute. Go in and rest, maybe have a cup of tea."

"Don't you get tired of doing all the work around here?"

"Hardly. I'd choose caring for a horse over a load of laundry any day."

Bethany crossed the yard, climbed the porch steps and sank into one of the rockers. Sarah walked out carrying two cups of tea and a tin of granola. "Say, you don't look so good," she said as she passed the cup of tea to Bethany.

"I wish people would stop saying that."

"Ah."

"*Danki* for the tea."

"Sure thing. How did work go today?"

Bethany shrugged, sipped the tea, eyed the granola but didn't reach for it. "Same as every other day."

"Yikes. This calls for more sugar." Sarah popped into the house and returned with a platter of oatmeal chocolate chip cookies.

Instead of reaching for one, Bethany set her tea cup on the small table, dropped her head into her hands and massaged her temples. When she finally looked up, Sarah was studying her, patiently waiting. Sarah was *gut* about that. She was *gut* about a lot of things.

"You should be married."

"That again?" Sarah reached for a cookie and grinned.

"You're a *wunderbaar* cook and a *gut* person, plus you're pretty. And your patience is a wonder to behold. Why aren't you married?"

"Honestly, I believe I missed my chance. Everyone my age is already paired up." She sounded disturbingly chipper at the thought. "But we were talking about you. More problems with Aaron?"

"How'd you guess?"

"You've been in something of a funk since he started working at the RV park."

"I suppose I have."

"So what has he done this time? Hung a resort sign over the entrance?"

Bethany laughed in spite of herself. "*Nein.* Not that. He worked on the community firepit all day. Can you imagine such a thing?"

"I can, actually. How do your guests like the games he set up?"

"Oh, they think everything Aaron does is fantastic. I'm subjected most of the day to the clang of horseshoes and shouts of victory from the washer pits."

"And your idea to give fresh-baked cookies to every camper?"

"Our guests were very appreciative."

"All right." Sarah sat back and ran a hand over the arm of the rocking chair. "Sounds as if you're at a bit of a stalemate regarding resort versus plain. So what else is bugging you?"

Bethany hesitated.

"Might as well get it off your heart and mind." Sarah's voice had turned from teasing to gentle.

Bethany never could resist Sarah when she wore that mothering look. "We had an argument, Aaron and I, at the wedding." She repeated what she could remember of it, which was practically every word because she'd gone over and over the conversation each day since—trying to figure out what she had to feel bad about.

Sarah didn't tell her that she shouldn't have lost her temper or that her words had been unkind. She didn't reprimand her in any way. Instead, she simply listened as Bethany relayed their argument, and then she picked up the plate of cookies.

"I think you have one more cookie delivery to make." She didn't wait for an answer. Instead, she stood and called out to Eunice. "No need to unhitch Oreo. Beth has an errand to run."

"Gotcha," Eunice called back.

And Bethany? She didn't argue, because Sarah, as usual, was right. She needed to make peace with Aaron. She needed to apologize for her harsh and defensive words. Driving toward his home, the plate of cookies on the seat beside her, she realized that she didn't have to like Aaron. She didn't have to enjoy being around him, but she did have to be kind so that she could sleep with a clear conscience.

She'd deliver the cookies with a smile and an apology.

Everything would return to how it was before—when they were simply adversaries and not enemies.

Everything would be fine.

She thought she knew where Aaron lived, but when she found Huckleberry Lane and turned on it, she wondered if she had the wrong place. The farms became ragtag—the houses looked to be a smattering of Amish and *Englisch*. All were in need of major repairs.

She turned toward what she thought was the King home. The drive was weedy, the bushes lining the lane in need of a good trimming. The fences surrounding the pastures looked as if they'd fall down in a good wind. The house at the end of the lane desperately needed a coat of paint, and the barn didn't look much better. She could see several patches on the roofs of both.

She called out to Oreo who obligingly stopped.

Did she have the right place?

Then she peered more closely at the field to her left. Small green buds were pushing through the soil. The rows were neat and recently plowed. Someone lived here.

"Walk on, Oreo."

As they approached the house, she saw Aaron's bike leaning against the barn wall. At least it looked like his bike. Then his *bruder*, Ethan, walked out of the barn and raised a hand in greeting. He reached out for Oreo's harness, talking pleasantly to the horse.

"Nice mare."

"Danki."

"Aaron's in the house if you're here to see him."

Bethany felt her cheeks blushing, but she held Ethan's gaze. She didn't remember him much from school. He was older than her. But he'd been pleasant at their church gatherings since he moved back. Two boys had left, and two men had returned. She wondered about that. Wondered why Esther King's only sons would move away.

"We had words at Becca's wedding. I brought a plate of Sarah's cookies as a peace offering."

"Looks as if I'll benefit from Aaron's bad manners then." He held the buggy door open, and she climbed out, plate in hand.

"I should only be a minute."

"No worries. I'll go in the barn and find... What's the mare's name?"

"Oreo."

"I'll find Oreo some treats. Take your time."

As Bethany walked toward the house, she was surprised to see an older man sitting in a rocker on the front porch. She supposed it must be Aaron's father, but she couldn't remember the last time she'd seen him. Today he looked washed-out and a bit dazed. He raised a hand in greeting as she skirted the holes in the porch steps and made her way to the front door.

She was about to knock on the door when Aaron jerked it open, looking startled to see her.

"Bethany."

"Aaron." She belatedly fixed a smile on her face. "I was hoping we could talk for a moment."

"Let me get my *dat* inside first." He walked over to his father, helped him to stand and then ushered him inside.

Bethany heard soft voices—Aaron and his *mamm*.

He returned outside and stood there on the porch, arms crossed, a sour look on his face.

"I…um…brought these cookies. Sarah made them. Oatmeal chocolate chip."

Aaron didn't smile. He also didn't reach for the plate.

And Bethany's good will snapped. "See, this is what I'm talking about. Even when I try to make a peace offering, you act as if I'm handing you a plate of chicken livers."

"What's wrong with chicken livers?"

She pretended to shiver, which caused him to at least smile. Aaron King was certainly a hard nut to crack.

Without another word, he took the plate of cookies from her, went back into the house and returned empty-handed. With a nod of his head, he indicated the west pasture fence. They walked there in silence—not necessarily companionable silence, but it wasn't as strained as the last few days had been.

The temperature was in the low sixties, the sun angling toward the horizon, and the mud from the four days of rain had begun to dry. Aaron stopped at the fence and draped his arms over it. Bethany had to stand on the bottom rung to do the same.

Finally he asked, "Why a peace offering?"

"Because I can't abide animosity in the work place."

He laughed. "I thought we just didn't like each other."

She tried to school her face, tried not to react, but some of the hurt must have leaked through.

"I didn't mean that." He hung his head, but then raised it, looked her straight in the eye. "I did not mean that. You're a very likable person."

"But…"

"But you and I didn't exactly get off to a good start."

"Oh, you mean because you tried to steal my job."

"*Ya*. That seemed to bother you from day one, for sure and certain."

She could have left it there. Things were better. They'd regained their equilibrium. But suddenly, to Bethany, it seemed a shame that they were merely tolerating each other.

"Becca worked in North Carolina last year—with MDS." She waited for Aaron to raise his eyes to hers. "The people in the floods, they lost everything quite suddenly. One moment everything was fine—it was raining, sure, but it didn't look so very different from any other rain. They went to bed feeling completely safe, feeling as if it were any other night during any other rainstorm. They woke to their homes being washed away."

Now he'd turned and was facing her, studying her, waiting.

Bethany stepped down off the fence slat and met

his straightforward gaze. "Life is short and unpredictable, *ya*? Maybe that's why I dislike conflict so much."

She almost stopped there but something prompted her to hold out her hand, as he had done to her that first day they'd worked together in the office. "Friends?"

He placed his hand in hers, shaking his head and smiling. "Friends."

She blushed at the feel of his fingers grasping her hand, which was stupid because it had been her idea. There was something about Aaron King that unsettled her. Perhaps it was his good looks—sandy blond hair brushing against his collar, blue eyes giving away nothing, strong broad shoulders that looked as if they could bear the weight of the world. Maybe it wasn't his looks at all, but rather the fact that she was never able to put her finger on what he was thinking. He was complicated and intriguing in a disconcerting way.

They turned and walked back toward the barn, where Oreo was patiently waiting.

"I'm sorry for losing my cool at the wedding." Aaron's apology sounded sincere, and the expression on his face was contrite. "The things I said were rude and uncalled for."

"And I'm sorry that I responded in kind."

Stopping next to Oreo, Aaron ran his hand down the mare's neck. Bethany thought about the man on the front porch when she'd first arrived. He'd been desperately pale, his hair uncombed, and dark circles had ringed his eyes. He'd looked too old to be Aaron's father. But Aaron had said—what was it?—*Let me get my dat inside first.*

"Is your *dat* okay? He looked...unwell."

Aaron hesitated.

She thought he'd brush her off, maybe make a joke or possibly return to his old standby—rudeness.

Instead he said, "My *dat* isn't well at all. He's been over in Middlebury these last few weeks and only returned home yesterday."

"I'm sorry, Aaron. I had no idea."

"It's not something we share with a lot of people. The bishop knows, of course, but that's about it."

"Were they able to help him? The doctors in Middlebury?" It had been obvious from the way the man had looked on the porch that they hadn't. Or possibly they had, and he'd been even worse before going there.

"They tried, but it's difficult to know if what they did worked, if it helped enough to actually make a difference now that he's returned home."

"I don't understand. Why did they send him home if he's not well?"

"Because he insisted. He always insists. He gets a little better, then comes home, then spirals downward. It's a cycle we've been through many times." He'd been staring at Oreo, but his gaze flicked up and settled on Bethany. "My *dat* has bipolar disorder. He's had it since before I was born. He'll always have it because there is no cure."

Chapter Seven

Aaron wasn't sure why the truth had come out of his mouth. He'd never once felt the urge to share the details of his *dat*'s disease with anyone. Today was different. Bethany was different, he realized. He somehow knew that he could trust her. And once he had, once he'd said those words—*my dat has bipolar disorder*—the look on Bethany's face assured him it was the right thing to do.

She didn't look shocked.

Her eyes didn't fill with pity.

She simply looked…concerned.

"That must be very hard on you, Aaron."

He shrugged. "*Ya*. I suppose."

"Do you want to talk about it?"

He stuck his hands in his pockets, moved a few steps away, then turned and walked to the bench positioned just outside the barn door. That old, tattered bench suddenly looked like a lifeboat on a dangerously stormy sea. He sank onto it, elbows on his legs, head bowed, fingers massaging his temples. He wasn't actually aware that Bethany had joined him until she placed a hand on his back and rubbed in slow, steady circles.

"I'm sorry…for what you're going through."

He sat up straighter and her hand fell away.

"As folks are fond of saying, *it is what it is.*"

"But—"

"But it isn't fair. Is it?" The old anger rose, and he thought he might choke on it. "My *bruder*, he reminds me that *Gotte* doesn't promise a life that's fair in the Good Book. That seems like a bad answer to me. It seems like no answer at all."

Bethany didn't argue with him, and that earned her even more points in his mind.

"What did you call it? Bipolar something?"

"Disorder. Bipolar disorder."

"I've never even heard of such a thing."

"Means that he goes high—" Aaron held his hand above his head, then dropped it to the ground "—and low."

"So he's moody?"

"Much more than that. When he's in the manic phase, the high phase, he has a lot of energy and a lot of strange ideas. His thoughts spin so quickly that he talks fast. Much of what he says doesn't make sense at all, and he won't listen to anyone. Then the paranoia sets in and his mood swings."

"What is that like?"

"You know how the barometric pressure falls just before a bad storm? It's like that. When he's in the depressed phase he gets sullen and angry."

Bethany's eyes were wide, and he could tell that she was listening—really listening—to what he had to say. He liked that she didn't attempt to brush it away with *I'm sure things will be fine* or *At least you have your mamm.* He'd heard both over the years. He'd heard worse.

After a moment where they simply sat there, backs against the barn, eyes on the far field, Bethany cleared her throat. "That's why you came back…why you and Ethan both came back?"

"It is."

"What happened?"

"He gave away what little money they had on some internet scam. He would sometimes go to town and use the computers at the library. Seems he'd set up some accounts, and he thought the business was legitimate. Even took a loan out against the farm."

"Did you tell the police?"

"We did. They're trying to locate the guilty party, but that's hard to do when the crime took place virtually. As for the money—it's gone."

"And the bank loans?"

"Due." Aaron let out a long breath. "He was in the manic phase when all of that happened. Then he plunged back down to the bottom, leaving *Mamm* to deal with the mess he'd made."

"So she called you and Ethan."

"And we came home." He should have felt worse, going over it again. He usually did feel worse in the wee hours of the morning when he couldn't sleep and he'd comb through the *how* and *why* of his ending up back on the decrepit farm.

This time was different though.

At least Ethan thought it could be, and just maybe his *bruder* was right.

Somehow, sharing his family's past with Bethany

made the load a little lighter. It wasn't as if she could do anything about it, but she was a good listener.

"Those loans he made, they're why you came to work at the market."

"And why I'm trying to do additional work on the side."

"What about the benevolence fund?"

"We'd rather not dip into that again, if it can be helped. We won't. If my parents lose the farm, maybe that isn't the worst thing that can happen. Maybe it will wake my *mamm* up. She tends to be protective of him. I'm not even sure that she fully accepts the permanence of his condition."

"What would you do then? If she lost the farm?"

Aaron shrugged. He assumed that he would go back to Sarasota and that Ethan would go back to Sugar Creek. But where would his parents go? That was a question he had shied away from even considering.

They stood and walked to Oreo, who was still patiently waiting. Horses were good about that—waiting, not pushing, accepting.

"*Danki*. For the cookies."

"*Gem gschehne.*"

The old words slipped between them, and for a moment, Aaron didn't feel different. He didn't feel out of place.

He watched Bethany drive away, knowing that nothing had really changed. They were still poor. The roofs of the barn and the house still leaked. His father's illness still overshadowed all else. And yet, Aaron found himself whistling as he walked toward the house.

Once in the kitchen, he saw that everyone else was already sitting down to dinner.

His *dat* shot him a glance. "Glad you could join us."

But his usual anger wasn't in the words, not yet. He was still fighting against the effects of the medication. He'd been on lithium, carbamazepine, even ziprasidone in the past. Aaron used to keep up with each prescription, reading the pamphlets that came with the bottles of medicine. Placing his hopes and even his future on the chance that one or the other or even a combination would work. So far, they hadn't.

They bowed their heads in silent prayer, a time to express gratitude for the simple meal in front of them—homemade soup, hot cornbread, fresh butter. That wasn't what Aaron prayed about though. In truth, he hadn't prayed a lot since receiving the call to come home. Maybe he'd been too angry. Maybe he simply hadn't known what to pray.

But something had changed.

As he smelled the aroma of potato soup and accepted the presence of his family around him, Aaron found he could pray. He found himself thanking *Gotte* for a plate of oatmeal cookies and the kind person who had brought it.

Everything changed after that. Bethany went straight home that night and shared with her family what was happening at the King home. For some reason, her *dat* didn't seem surprised. Perhaps the bishop had told him a little of the situation. Maybe that's why he'd hired Aaron. Regardless, he wouldn't keep him on as an employee unless he pulled his weight at the market—something that Aaron was determined to do.

She found herself looking forward to work in the mornings. Sarah began packing a little extra food for her, and Bethany had it set out by the coffee pot when Aaron walked into the office. She also made sure that they had instant coffee on hand.

Aaron always praised the food, and he thanked her for remembering the coffee.

They were nearing the end of April, and the days were warmer now. They'd begun walking through the RV park together each morning—after they'd had coffee and cookies or sweet rolls or coffee cake. Bethany and Aaron would walk up and down the lanes of the RV park calling out to the campers, stopping to see if there was anything they needed.

A short storm had blown through, causing more limbs to fall. Aaron spent a full day cutting up the wood and stacking it next to the site of the new community firepit. Bethany had no desire to learn to use a chainsaw, though she suspected Eunice would enjoy doing so. She realized—not for the first time—that it was a big help to have Aaron around. Perhaps her *dat*'s idea of being co-managers wasn't such a bad one.

On Friday of the week after their discussion about Aaron's *dat*, they were walking through the RV park when Aaron led her toward the firepit and held both arms out wide. "All finished. What do you think of it?"

"I think it's amazing. I didn't picture anything nearly this nice."

Aaron smiled broadly at the praise, but that wasn't why she'd said it. At least it wasn't the only reason why. The firepit *was* amazing. Aaron had done a very good job. The circular area was bordered by a wall of interlocking bricks. When she sat down on one, she was pleased to find that it was quite steady. No chance of a brick falling over while a child sat on it.

In the center of the pit was a small pile of logs set up in a cone shape. A few feet away from the pit, Aaron had built a place to stack wood. It was even covered to keep the wood dry when it rained. He'd also penned a waterproof sign that read, *Feel free to enjoy our simple firepit!*

"I see you worked the word *simple* into your sign."

"That I did. Someone keeps reminding me that this is an Amish establishment."

"Our guests are going to love this. I would like to officially admit that I was wrong and you were right."

Aaron stumbled backward and clutched his chest, then he started laughing. "Don't hear that from a woman every day."

She swiped at him, but he caught her hand, squeezed it and smiled. Good grief, he was a handsome man. Why did she keep noticing that?

"We should stay late tonight and try it out," he suggested. "Have a s'mores party."

Bethany thought she should say no. It sounded too cozy, too intimate. Then she chided herself for letting her thoughts drift that direction. Aaron wasn't asking her out on a date, and they'd be surrounded by families of campers.

"Sure. That sounds fun. I'll just tell my *dat* I won't be needing a ride home."

They were nearly back at the office when Aaron stopped in his tracks. "Wait. If you don't ride with your *dat*, how will you get home? I don't think riding double on my bike is an option."

Oops. She hoped what she was about to tell him didn't set off fireworks. "Actually, I've been riding my bike to work in the mornings, then *dat* loads it on the back of the buggy in the afternoons, and I ride home with him."

Aaron studied her a minute, then walked up the steps to the office, stopped to stamp his feet on the mat before going inside, sending a *See, I can learn new tricks* smile back at her. He plopped down into the chair, crossed his arms and said, "Explain yourself, woman. Why would you ride your bike to work when you can ride with your *dat* in a nice buggy?"

"Okay. It's not what you're thinking."

"What was I thinking?"

"Actually, I have no idea."

She walked over to their mini fridge, pulled out a can of soda and wiggled it at him.

"Sure. Why not? It'll make whatever you're about to say go down easier."

She snagged another for herself, took her time walking around the desk and plopped down in her seat. "Okay. What I meant to say is that I didn't start riding my bike because you're riding yours."

He raised his eyebrows, popped the top on the soda and took a long drink, staring up at the ceiling while he drank. Finally he returned his gaze to her. Bethany wanted to press the coldness of the can she was holding against her flaming cheeks, but she didn't want to admit she was embarrassed. As if he couldn't see! She was acting like a schoolgirl who'd been caught doodling some boy's name on her notebook.

She cleared her throat, opened the soda, and took a small sip. "Yes, seeing you ride your bike to work did start me thinking."

"About?"

"About how I take things for granted. If my *dat* didn't

work here, I'd be riding a bike…so then that led me to wondering if I'd like it. You know—exercise in the morning and everything."

"And have you…liked it?"

She finally relaxed back in the chair. "*Ya*. Surprisingly, I have. It's…it's nice to be alone with my thoughts for a few minutes. Not that my *dat* is a chatterbox, but still, we do usually end up talking about family or work."

"But not if you ride your bike to town."

"Exactly—it provides a little 'me time.'" She put the last two words in air quotes. "You might be surprised to hear it, but I've always been a bit of an introvert."

"You don't say?"

"Now you're mocking me."

"You threw up before you gave your report in seventh grade."

"You remember that?"

"I do." He continued to study her for a moment and finally said, "You don't strike me as an introvert now."

"You wouldn't say that if you saw me at home. I'm always the quiet one."

"But here…"

His grin often reminded her of the Cheshire cat; only this time, she found it rather adorable.

"Oh, *nein*. Here I'm outgoing and always pleasant."

"Unless someone tracks mud on your rug."

They both smiled at the memory. "Seems like a long time ago," she murmured.

It was settled. The first s'more gathering of the Plain & Simple RV Resort was to take place at dusk.

Bethany went and spoke to her *dat* while Aaron walked around the RV park informing the customers about the impromptu s'more party. Her *dat* thought it was a *gut* idea, but he refused to even consider allowing her to ride her bike home after dark.

"You could get run over by an *Englischer*. I've even seen Amish youngsters almost drive their buggy off the road staring down at the cell phone they're not supposed to have. *Nein*. You take the buggy and take Aaron home too."

"But how will you—"

Her *dat* waved away her concerns. "There are a lot of employees here. Surely I can catch a ride with one of them."

The rest of the day flew by. Bethany and Aaron had a little time to kill between the end of the workday and dark, so they walked through the half dozen streets of downtown Shipshe, stopped and had dinner at the pizzeria and then walked to the town's small grocer to purchase the graham crackers, chocolate bars and marshmallows.

Bethany stopped in front of a display of cooking utensils. Metal skewers were sixteen dollars for a package of eight. They'd need a lot more than eight. She turned to Aaron, who was already shaking his head.

"What?"

"That would be the *Englisch* way. We're plain, remember?"

He was teasing her again, but instead of irking her Bethany found that she rather liked it. "Okay. So, what are we going to put the marshmallows on?"

"I found a box of old wire clothes hangers in the supply shed. No idea where those came from, but figured they would be okay to use. We'll need to unbend them, maybe snip them in half."

Which was what they did for the remaining hour.

They were situated next to the firepit by half past seven. Bethany was a little nervous that perhaps no one would come, but first one camper, then another showed up, carrying lawn chairs and wearing a smile. In the end, they had to scooch closer together so that everyone would fit in the circle.

Aaron's cone-shaped stack of wood worked perfectly. When he set a match to it, the entire thing began blazing in no time at all. Soon they'd passed around the hangers, now shaped into s'more sticks, as well as the marshmallows.

It seemed that everyone had a particular way they liked to roast their marshmallow. Some took their time and waited for it to turn a light brown. Others stuck it into the flames, watched it blaze, then blew it out, leaving a black crust.

Of course, Bethany liked hers a soft brown, and Aaron preferred his burnt. She accepted a piece of chocolate bar from Aaron, stacked it on a graham cracker, then added her perfectly toasted marshmallow and the top graham cracker. It looked too large to eat.

Aaron leaned closer and said in a mock whisper, "Smoosh it together, and you can actually take a bite," which caused everyone to laugh.

The first bite took Bethany back to her childhood. How long had it been since she'd done this? And why had they ever stopped? The chocolate was warm, the marshmallow gooey and the crackers crisp. She groaned.

"I know, right?" Aaron bumped his shoulder against hers.

The older folks laughed and talked about when they

were a child, when roasting marshmallows was a regular Friday night event.

The parents with young children had to show them how it was done, and though the boys and girls were sticky and hyped up on sugar, they were smiling by the time they were hustled off to bed.

One by one, their guests said goodnight, followed by "Let's do this again" and "Wonderful idea" and "This place is starting to feel like home." That last comment really pricked Bethany's heart, because it was what she'd wanted all along—for their guests to consider the RV park their second home.

It took less than ten minutes to clean up the supplies, and then she and Aaron were walking across the now empty parking lot to her *dat*'s buggy. Employee buggies were all parked in one area, adjacent to a field where the horses could spend their day. The teenaged boy working that corner of the parking lot always unhitched the horses when employees arrived. If he saw you walking back toward him at the end of the day, he'd usually fetch the horse from the field and help with the harness.

Someone had already done that for Peanut, who was standing there looking as if she'd been catching a nap.

"Hmmm… Oreo seems to have changed colors on us."

"Oreo is our old family horse. She's as much a pet as a buggy horse. This is Peanut. She's only been with us a couple of years."

"*Ya*? Well, it looks as if she didn't mind staying a bit late."

"*Nein*. Peanut is always up for a little late-night fun." She had no idea why she said that. She couldn't remember the last time she'd been out after dark, and in fact, it wasn't dark now. Almost though. The light was nearly gone, and she could see the first few stars in the sky. She thought of making a wish. What would she wish for? What did she want?

"I'll just hitch up my bike beside yours."

"There are bungee cords in the box."

"Got it."

As Aaron fastened his bike to the back of the buggy, Bethany stood talking to the mare. She hesitated to get in the buggy. She didn't know if she should offer to drive or ask him to. She blew out a breath. "I have no idea what I'm doing here, Peanut."

She didn't realize that Aaron was directly behind her until he said in a soft, low voice. "I suppose you should drive since you're dropping me off."

"Oh, right." She spun around, but Aaron didn't back up.

Instead, he looked down at her, and in that moment, the world seemed to tilt. Bethany had the strangest feeling of standing apart, watching what was about to happen. She might have stopped Aaron, stepped away, looked down, given any kind of signal that she wasn't interested. But she was interested. She realized that in the instant before he put a finger under her chin, tilted her face up and then kissed her softly on the lips.

She hadn't been ready for that. Her lips felt tingly, and her heart was beating like she'd run a mile.

Aaron was grinning as he stepped back. "I guess our first s'more night was a success."

"Oh, I agree. Some reporter will probably do a write-up in the *Shipshewana Daily News* about us."

As they drove toward Aaron's home, they talked about

work, about the RV park, about what summer would be like once the market opened.

Neither mentioned the kiss.

But Bethany was thinking about it.

When she pulled onto Huckleberry Lane, he stayed her hand. "You don't have to drive me up. Just let me out here."

She wondered if he was embarrassed to be seen with her.

Then she noticed his gaze flicker down the lane toward the house, toward his family. He wasn't embarrassed. He was choosing a quiet approach. Had his entire life been like that…constantly tiptoeing around his *dat*?

"How is he doing?"

"Less sleepy than when he first came home. Talking faster, too much energy."

"That's bad, right?"

"*Ya*. In the past it has been."

"Is there anything you can do?"

"He has an appointment with his doctor next week. Hopefully they'll get him back on track."

"And if they don't?"

"Then we'll just have to wait and see what he manages to wreck next…and try to stay out of the way." He reached over, squeezed her hand, then hopped out of the buggy. She listened to him retrieve his bicycle. He offered her a final wave, then turned and walked the bike slowly down the lane into the darkness. He was apparently in no hurry to get home, and she didn't blame him.

She thought of that as she drove home. She hadn't had a normal childhood, because her *mamm* had died when she was so young, and her *dat* had never remarried. But she'd always felt that their house was a safe place—a place where she was loved and where the people there cared about her.

As she drove home, she wondered what he meant by *we*.

He'd said, *We'll just have to wait and see what he manages to wreck next…*

Who had he meant with the word *we*? Probably, he was referring to himself and Ethan, but just maybe he included her in that group. She hoped he did. She hoped that he understood she was on his side.

And then her mind returned to wondering about that kiss.

Chapter Eight

The Plain community in Shipshe held church services on the second and fourth Sunday of each month. The first and third Sundays were open to allow members to visit family in surrounding districts—often attending church with them. It made it easier to go to baptisms or visit for birthdays. When families weren't attending their own service or a nearby service, they held a morning Bible reading in their home, then joined a few nearby families for lunch.

The Bible readings in Aaron's home had never been something he looked forward to. Sometimes his *dat* was in his manic phase—in which case there was an agitated overly focused feel to the prayers and Bible study. Other times, he was in his depressed phase and sat in an armchair, eyes downcast, saying very little.

If other families invited them over for luncheon, his *mamm* had—in the past—always found a reason to say no.

The Sunday after he'd kissed Bethany was different in one way and the same in another. It was different because Bishop Ezekiel had invited them to lunch, and apparently Esther hadn't been able to come up with a valid excuse not to attend. It was the same because Aaron's *dat* was once more spiraling upward into his manic phase.

Throughout breakfast, their *dat* talked about a dream he'd had which he interpreted to mean that they should stop attempting to raise crops and start raising emus.

"The crops are already in the ground, *dat*. We won't be pulling them out." Ethan kept his voice light, but he didn't leave room for argument. He did exchange a solemn glance with Aaron. They both knew that the storm was on the horizon. Their *dat* wasn't likely to accept *no* for an answer.

Zackary King's sons had never argued with him before, never contradicted him in any way, and he wasn't happy that they'd chosen today to start doing so.

He clenched and unclenched his big hands, as if he were loosening up the muscles there. The veins in his neck stood out as he lifted his chin and attempted to stare down his oldest son. When Ethan didn't back down, didn't respond in any way, he turned to Aaron. His eyes narrowed into a piercing stare, and his voice sounded as if he were having to force the words through a very narrow space. "Do you agree with your *bruder*?"

"*Ya*, I do." Aaron was surprised to find that his voice didn't shake at all. In fact, he found his father's whole act to be rather pitiful, but certainly not threatening. "The crops are coming in well. We tried to show you, but you refused to walk to the—"

Zackary slammed his fist on the table, causing the dishes to bounce and clatter. Pointing a fork toward Aaron then Ethan, he growled, "If I remember correctly, the Good Book says to honor your parents. I'll thank you to remember I'm the parent here."

Aaron's heart hammered against his chest. The peace and assuredness of the moment before vanished. It was as if his body betrayed his mind. As if his breathing and heart and muscles didn't realize that he was now an adult, that he had nothing to fear from this man who was so obviously out of control.

Conversely, Ethan continued to appear calm and unperturbed. "Perhaps you should remember that we're about to lose this farm thanks to your gambling."

"I will not tolerate your insolence." Zackary pushed his plate away, having barely tasted the food. He sat back, crossed his arms and scowled at his sons. "You wonder why I don't want to be seen in public with either one of you. It's because you make me sick. It's because you don't know how to be proper sons."

Ethan wasn't backing down. "Perhaps we could talk to Bishop Ezekiel about your concerns this afternoon—when we visit him for lunch."

"I'm not going to that luncheon just so you all can gang up on me." Zackary picked up his coffee cup, looking at it as if he'd never seen it before.

Aaron thought that perhaps he would drink the fresh coffee, maybe the caffeine would work to change his mood. But they never found out because his *dat* hurled the coffee cup across the room. It hit the opposite wall and shattered, leaving shards of ceramic on the floor and coffee dripping down the wall.

The day was spiraling out of control as so many others had, and it wasn't yet seven in the morning. Aaron wanted to groan and drop his head in his hands. He

wanted to pack his few sets of clothes into his backpack
and walk out the door—walk away and never look back.

And then something else happened that never had
happened before. His *mamm* touched her napkin to her
lips, placed it gingerly beside her plate and then looked
directly at her husband. "We will *all* be going to the
bishop's for luncheon—including you, Zackary. The
terms of his helping us this time, helping *you*, was that
you not self-isolate. We won't be staying home and pretending life is normal. We will go to that luncheon, and
if you'd like to speak to Ezekiel about your ideas for
animals, then you're more than welcome to do that."

She actually smiled softly, and Aaron realized in
that moment that despite all his *dat* had done, she still
loved him. How did love survive years of abuse and
neglect and poverty? He couldn't say that he loved his
dat. He mostly felt remorse, sadness, even anger when
he thought of him—but not love.

Zackary stood, roughly pushed back his chair, causing it to fall over, and stormed from the room.

They didn't see him again the rest of the morning.

Aaron helped his *mamm* clean up the shattered cup
and dripping coffee. The three of them held a short
Bible study in the sitting room. Ethan had chosen Ex-
odus 14:14. "The Lord will fight for you, and ye shall
hold your peace."

Maybe so. Maybe Moses was right, and the Lord had
fought for the Israelites. Aaron only knew that an hour
ago in their kitchen, he'd felt rather on his own. And
yet, he was commanded to hold his peace? He shook his
head in confusion and bowed his head when Ethan and
his *mamm* prayed, but he was pretty sure any words he

uttered to the Lord stopped at the roof that still leaked whenever it rained.

When it was time to leave, Ethan brought the buggy around—Misty harnessed and looking indifferent as to whether they went any farther than the lane. To Aaron's surprise, his *dat* walked to the buggy without argument. But he insisted on sitting in the back. "My son knows more than I do, so he should drive."

Aaron was relieved that his *mamm* sat in the back with *Dat*. It meant that he could ride up front with Ethan. He took a deep breath as Misty trotted down Huckleberry Lane. He tried to focus on the spring weather, the green crops, the day of rest. He failed. Everything outside the buggy passed by in a blur. All he could see was the scene in the kitchen playing on a loop through his mind.

The short drive was a silent one. Ethan directed the mare into Bishop Ezekiel's place. Several buggies were already there, and Aaron recognized one of the Yoder's mares—Peanut—in the pasture.

"Didn't realize the Yoder family would be attending," Ethan said in a low voice. "That's *gut*, right?"

"I suppose."

"You and Bethany worked out your differences?"

Aaron thought of the kiss they'd shared. "You could say that."

At first, he didn't notice anything different about the gathering. Nathan Troyer, the older guy Gideon had lived with, was there as well as Gideon's *bruder*, Luke. It was a small group, and that should have helped to settle his nerves, but it didn't. He found himself keeping an eye on his *dat*. Throughout the meal, Aaron's *dat* spoke too loudly, throwing up his arms to make a point, laughing robustly over a joke that deserved at best a small smile.

But slowly Aaron became aware that something else was going on. Something had changed, but he couldn't put his finger on what.

Before the meal, Bethany's *dat* had made a point to seek him out and say, "We're all praying for your family, Aaron. You come and see me if I can do anything."

During the meal, when they were talking about the coming crowds expected at the market, Gideon had said, "We'll all be working a full forty hours."

Then he'd glanced at Aaron and said, "Of course, if you need time off for family reasons, we can work around that."

It was when Ada clumsily patted his arm and said, "I know family can make you crazy sometimes. Mine makes me pull my *kapp* off my head at times, I'm so frustrated, but remember…home is where the feet are."

Ada's sayings never made much sense to him, but it was more than that. He was certain something was up.

Then he saw Bethany standing near her *schweschder* Eunice and looking his way. He saw Eunice squeeze Bethany's hand, then smile his direction and offer a small wave. And he finally understood. The temper that he'd been trying to hold on to all morning reached a boiling point. He knew that he should wait, take a deep breath and calm down before he approached her.

He should, but he didn't.

Bethany smiled as Aaron walked toward her. She smiled until she saw the expression on his face. *Uh-oh.* Something was up, and it wasn't good.

He stood in front of her, arms crossed, a scowl causing wrinkles to form between his eyes. "What did you do?"

"What did I do?"

"Did you tell everyone?"

"Tell them…"

"What I shared with you! What I shared in private, Bethany—details about my *dat*'s condition and what Ethan and *mamm* and I are dealing with at home. Did you tell your entire family? Did you tell…" His words stuttered and his arm shot out waving toward the group still sitting under the trees. "Did you tell everyone?"

She opened her mouth to speak, shut it, then looked around. A few people were throwing glances their way. She reached for his arm. When he pulled away, she stepped closer. "Unless you want everyone to know we're fighting, you should walk with me. We could go and check out Bishop Ezekiel's sheep and have a private conversation. If that's what you want."

He narrowed his eyes, but he didn't pull away as she slipped her hand through the crook of his arm. They walked past the barn. Once they had moved out of sight of the others, he stepped away—put some space between them as if she had a contagious disease. She didn't press, didn't ask questions. She wanted to give him a few moments to sort his feelings. It was obvious that he was upset about something, upset at her about something.

They walked to the pasture fence. Merino sheep of all sizes dotted the field. The lambs that had been born six weeks earlier were frolicking about, darting away from their *mamm* and then back again. Sunlight shone down on the field that was resplendent with grass and wildflowers. The blueness of the sky made Bethany's eyes water. It was a beautiful day, a *wunderbaar* Lord's Day, but the man beside her wasn't seeing that at all.

He finally turned toward her, his hands clenched at his side. "I can't believe that you shared something I told you in private, in confidence."

"Okay. I'm sorry. I didn't realize that you wouldn't want my family to know."

"I've spent my entire life not wanting anyone to know."

Now her temper rose to match his. Bethany didn't get angry often, but when she did, it always felt as if steam were pouring out of her ears. She turned toward him, planting her feet and fisting her hands on her hips. "And maybe that's part of the problem."

"What's that supposed to mean?"

"It means that when you keep something a secret, no one can help you."

"Maybe I don't want their help. Maybe I don't want their pity." He turned, stomped off half a dozen steps, then reversed course back toward her. The fight had gone out of him. His shoulders slumped and he couldn't quite meet her gaze. Instead he stared at his shoes. His voice, when he spoke, held such a tone of despair that it caused her heart to ache.

"You had no right to share what I told you in confidence. If I had wanted everyone to know the ins and outs of my *dat*'s condition, I would have taken out an ad in *The Budget*."

He threw her a look of disgust, worse yet of disappointment, and then he was gone. She saw very little of him the next hour. Though luncheons usually lasted well into the afternoon and it was barely past two, she jerked her head toward the lane when she heard the sound of buggy wheels. Aaron and his family were trun-dling toward the road, away from the small gathering.

No one mentioned their early departure.

No one commented on Aaron's sullen mood or his *dat*'s manic behavior. At least it had seemed manic to Bethany. She thought back over what Aaron had told her—about the highs followed by the lows. Manic epi-sodes followed by depressed ones. How had he put it? *We'll just have to wait and see what he manages to wreck next...and try to stay out of the way.*

She couldn't imagine such a life.

She was still upset with Aaron for unfairly berating her, but she also felt sympathy for him. Her heart felt sore thinking of what Aaron and his *bruder* and his *mamm* were going through. She even felt compassion for his father, who seemed to her like a ship tossed on a turbulent sea. The problem was that his tossing about hurt others.

Bethany's family had arrived in two buggies. Becca, Gideon and her *dat* rode in the buggy with the new mare, Kit Kat. Bethany found it impossible to look at Kit Kat and not smile. The mare looked so inordinately pleased with the day, the buggy she pulled, even with herself. She was a mare full of confidence.

Bethany rode with her *schweschdern* in the buggy pulled by Peanut, who also seemed delighted by the day. Sarah waited until they were on the way home to ask her about what had happened. Bethany was sit-ting up front with her oldest *schweschder*; Eunice and Ada were in the back seat. Eunice was doodling a new idea on a scrap of paper, but she stuffed it in her purse when Sarah said, "Tell us what happened with you and Aaron."

Both Eunice and Ada moved to the middle of the back seat so that they could peer over and catch every word.

"Aaron looked as mad as a wet chicken." Ada grimaced. "He definitely was not happy."

"*Nein*. He wasn't." Bethany tried to decide how much she should say. After all, he was upset that she'd shared anything with her family about him. Would this make things worse? But that didn't seem possible. After all, he was already out of sorts with her. She'd always turned to her family for advice, and she didn't plan on stopping now.

So she told them why he was angry. Sarah tossed a glance her way, then returned her attention to the road. "It's a difficult situation, for sure and certain. And Aaron has spent all of his life convinced things would be better if no one knew the details of what was happening at home."

"Hard to teach a young mare new tricks." Ada looked so serious that Bethany couldn't bring herself to correct her.

It was what Eunice said that poked Bethany's heart, because it mirrored exactly what she'd been thinking.

"I can't imagine growing up like that—with so much uncertainty and volatility in your home." She shook her head. "And it was obvious that his *dat* was agitated today. I might not have noticed it if you hadn't shared his condition with us, but now that I know…well, it was fairly obvious that he's still struggling."

And there it was.

Aaron was no doubt truly upset with her, but he was more upset with his *dat*. He was once again enduring the highs and lows of his father's condition. He was working hard, but his *dat* could still manage to put everything—all of the progress they'd made—in danger. Eunice was correct. Such a life was difficult to imagine.

"We already all know now, so there's no going back." Sarah pulled on the rein to turn Peanut into their lane.

The horse looked every bit as happy to be home as she had to be on the road—head high, ears perked up, tail swishing. Life was fairly simple if you were a horse, or so it seemed to Bethany.

Sarah reached over and squeezed Bethany's hand. "What we can do is pray for Aaron and Ethan and their parents, and try to be *gut* friends."

"If they'll let us." To Bethany, that didn't seem very likely now. She hadn't meant to hurt Aaron, but she had. No doubt, he regretted the kiss they'd shared. She suspected he was sorry he had let his guard down with her.

But the conversation with her *schweschdern* helped. Bethany understood that while Aaron's anger might be directed at her, it was actually more about the course his life kept taking. His accusations had hurt her feelings—she didn't bother denying that to herself. She cared about him, as a friend, and she didn't want to see him miserable. It was okay that he'd lashed out. Sometimes friends did that to someone they could trust. What mattered—as far as their friendship was concerned—was that he didn't act that way normally. He was a patient, kind, pleasant guy. That was the real Aaron—the one who managed to break free of his family's history.

So she didn't waste any time or energy replaying his hurtful words.

She prayed for patience and for understanding.

She vowed to be a better friend, if he would let her.

And she pushed away any thoughts of the kiss. It was more than obvious that Aaron was not ready for a relationship of any kind.

Chapter Nine

Aaron should have been prepared—mentally—for the opening-day crowds. He wasn't. Over seven hundred vendors were set up and ready for business. Amos had hired someone to be a night watchman on Monday and Tuesday evenings—an *Englisch* gentleman named Brody, who apparently was a retired police officer. Each vendor booth had electricity and free Wi-Fi. The market was pet friendly, which meant vendors as well as shoppers brought along their animals. He saw quite a few dogs and the occasional cat, bird or rabbit.

On days the market was open, Shipshewana often saw as many as thirty-five thousand guests. For a town of less than seven hundred, that was a lot of people. His and Bethany's workweek had officially changed to Tuesday through Saturday, but they'd both worked on Monday since it was the day before opening. Aaron didn't mind the overtime, and Amos had made it clear that he expected everyone to be there.

It had been a difficult day. He'd spent most of it avoiding Bethany and trying to help with the market vendors—which wasn't technically in his list of responsibilities, but he was willing to lend a hand wherever it was needed. Gideon had briefed all the workers at a large luncheon the day before. Aaron had listened and thought he understood, but imagining so many people and seeing so many were two different things. The market would be open every Tuesday and Wednesday through September. That was in addition to the antique auction every Wednesday, the livestock auction every Wednesday and the horse auction every Friday—all year-round events.

He'd barely spent any time in the RV park on Monday, so Tuesday he arrived early. Vendors had apparently arrived at the market sometime near sunup. The official opening time was 8:00 a.m., but when Aaron pedaled to the back of the parking area at 7:30 a.m., there was already a line of cars filled with shoppers and tourists waiting their turn to pull into the parking area.

Like the rest of the market, the RV park was full. Apparently, a lot of people made it part of their annual pilgrimage to be at the market on opening day. Everyone appeared to be in high spirits, calling out hello as Aaron made his way over to the supply shed. The last thing he wanted to do was go into the office. He was not ready to face Bethany again. One part of him knew that he'd overreacted, but another part felt as if he was justified in his anger. He felt betrayed. He'd thought that Bethany was his friend, had even entertained daydreams that she might be more than that. Now he understood such thoughts were merely sandcastles in the sky. She couldn't understand his life. Why would she even want to?

It didn't help that the situation at home had worsened since the Sunday luncheon.

He didn't want to dwell on that this fine Tuesday morning though. The crowded parking lot, throngs of people and the smell of sizzling food might have raised his spirits, but he was rather determined to be in a slump. Working always helped. His plan was to begin the task of building the gazebo. A portion of the materials had been delivered the Friday before. He would need help once he reached the actual construction phase, but for now, he could measure off the space, level the ground and begin cutting the boards to the proper length.

He was doing that, using the electric saw to cut the boards he'd measured for the base, when Bethany appeared. She looked rested and pretty, but he scowled at her nonetheless. She waited for him to finish the cut he was working on, then stepped forward.

"I didn't realize you were starting this today."

He raised the eye goggles to the top of his head. "Did you have something else I needed to do?"

"Well, it's all rather chaotic since this is our first day open."

"Not *our* first day though—the RV park has been open all along."

"Still, our park is rather full."

"What do you need me to do, Bethany?"

She pulled a piece of paper from her pocket. "Site twenty-one is having trouble with their sewer hose reaching to the trap. Thirty-four would like you to help them tie up a rope from one tree to another for a dog run."

He sighed heavily, unplugged the saw, set it on the workbench and tossed his goggles there as well. "Fine. Is that all?" He stepped forward to take the paper from her, then stepped away. The more distance between them, the better.

"Last night's wind blew the McDaniel's table umbrella into the creek. They were wondering if you could fetch it for them."

He put his hands on his hips and stared at the ground.

All three were things that he could take care of, but what was Bethany doing all day? Knitting in the office? Embroidering some nonsensical saying onto a bit of cloth? Drinking coffee and eating Sarah's coffee cake? They weren't exactly fair thoughts for him to entertain, and he knew that. He wanted to be unhappy today. He'd worked himself into a terrible mood, and he knew it. He shouldn't be judging her.

Bethany took care of reservations, accepted payments and answered guests' questions. She even provided maps and directions for places folks wanted to visit in the area. Some days her office had guests in it from the moment the little office opened until the moment it closed.

He scowled at the paper again. She hated anything that had to do with sewers. There was no way she could tie a dog lead up in a tree. The umbrella—she could probably handle that, so why had she asked him to do it? He didn't want to ask. He didn't want to have that conversation, or any conversation, with Bethany Yoder. He wanted to hold on to his anger, and it was hard to do that when she was standing there looking fresh and pretty, patiently waiting, a small smile on her lips, concern in her eyes.

"I'll take care of them."

"*Danki*, Aaron." She waited and finally added, "I can see you're still upset, and I want to say I'm sorry."

"Sorry doesn't always cut it." He reached for his straw hat, slapped it onto his head and stormed off.

He was being unreasonable.

He knew that.

But he had to let off steam somewhere, or he was going to explode. Who could he talk to about the way that his life lurched from disaster to disaster? No one, because the one person he'd trusted had turned out to be unreliable.

He helped the guests in site twenty-one with the sewer hose. They needed an extension, and he kept plenty of those in the supply shed. Affixing the dog run in the tree for site thirty-four took less than twenty minutes, but the old gent wanted to talk. By the time he'd finished with both of those, his stomach was growling.

He set off to find lunch.

Over the course of the last few weeks, he'd taken to eating with Bethany in the small office, but that was no longer an option. He walked up and down the vendor aisles and settled on buying a hot dog, chips and soda from the canteen. He shouldn't have spent the money, but the way things were going at home, it wouldn't matter. Saving a little money here and there was not going to solve their problems.

His *dat* was in full free fall. All the symptoms were there. He was determined to find a way to destroy their plans. The details didn't matter as much as the fact that he would be the one in charge. He'd moved on from raising emus to planting herbs for a natural supplement company that he'd read about on the library computers. Apparently, Aaron's *mamm* had left him there while she ran errands. An idle hour in his father's hands quickly turned into a new direction for his flights of fancy and a long lecture at the dinner table.

Aaron could practically hear the countdown clock ticking its way to the next meltdown, the next emergency, the final straw that would break his and Ethan's plan for financial recovery.

He walked back to the RV park, purposely ignoring all of the people around him. They were too cheerful, too obviously living a life that he would never have. He spent the rest of the afternoon cutting boards and stacking them in piles. The actual building of the gazebo could begin the next day—provided Bethany didn't come up with more campsite emergencies.

He'd worked later than he intended, and the sun was nearly down by the time he made it to the parking area where he stored his bike. The market was blessedly quiet now. He couldn't imagine that many people would be there again the next day. Perhaps it was a one-time thing.

His bike was in the same area where workers parked their buggies, adjacent to the field where the horses were pastured. He stopped next to the bike rack, not really surprised that his was the only one still there. But something else was off. He stood there a moment, trying to figure out what was bothering him. He looked from the single remaining buggy to the horse in the field—it was Oreo. There was no doubt about it.

Why was Bethany still here?

Where was Bethany?

He turned in a full circle. Only one car was left in the parking area, and it probably belonged to the night watchman. No other vehicles. No other buggies. Something wasn't adding up. Why would Bethany still be here? Or perhaps Amos was the one working late.

Aaron walked to the office, but it was closed up tight. Amos must have driven the other buggy, or perhaps he'd ridden with Gideon. It didn't make any sense. The first day had exhausted everyone, and all the employees were gone.

He saw Brody, the night watchman, walking the perimeter, and he waved a hand in acknowledgment, then he turned back to the RV park. Walking up to the little building, he had a sense of foreboding. Bethany wasn't in the office, but neither was it locked. He stepped around the desk and opened the bottom drawer. Her purse was still there. She hadn't left for home.

So where was she?

He hadn't seen her since she'd shown up asking for his help.

He hadn't eaten lunch with her, hadn't offered to bring her back anything. In fact, he hadn't spoken to her since he'd been so rude about helping the campers.

Aaron stepped out of the office, scanning the area, looking for any sign of her. He'd taken care of the sewer hose and the dog lead. What else had she asked him to do? Something about an umbrella. He snapped his fingers—the McDaniel's umbrella. He'd forgotten about that. Had she taken care of it herself? Could Bethany be visiting with them? Maybe she had lost track of the time.

He didn't think so though.

Bethany was friendly and personable with guests, but she didn't usually pull up a chair and share a cup of coffee. Still, it was the only idea he had. He headed toward the back of the RV park, found the McDaniel's RV and knocked on the door.

"*Ya*. She stopped by here an hour or so ago to see if we'd fetched it." Justin McDaniel was eighty, if he was a day. "Haven't seen her since then."

"And the umbrella blew into the creek?"

"I believe so, but it can wait until tomorrow. There's no hurry. We won't be using it tonight."

"I'll just check and see if I can spot it."

The RV park backed up to a seasonal creek, and the McDaniel's site was positioned next to that. The embankment dropped about seven feet. He peered into the ravine and saw that the water level was low, as usual, probably less than a foot deep. The sun had nearly set, but there was still enough light for him to see down into the creek as he walked its length.

He stayed up top, walking along the edge of the embankment.

Aaron couldn't have even said what he was looking for, but dread had filled his stomach and sweat beaded on his forehead.

He nearly gave up, sure that there was no umbrella and no Bethany, when he reached a bend and saw a red-and-white checked cloth…and beside it?

There was Bethany lying in the mud, eyes closed, her arm bent at an unnatural angle.

Bethany woke to a blinding headache and Aaron peering down at her, shaking her shoulder, begging her to open her eyes.

Why did her left arm hurt so badly? She turned her head, her eyes widening as she saw that it was swollen and turned at a strange direction. She promptly turned her head the other direction and threw up.

"Hey. Look at me, Bethany. You're okay. Do you hear me?"

Aaron was kneeling beside her now, pulling back her *kapp* strings, placing a reassuring hand on her back. "Don't look at your arm. Look at me, Beth."

Hearing her pet name, the name that only her family ever used, brought her attention back to Aaron. She turned her face toward him, met his gaze, and realized that the Aaron she knew and cared for was back. There wasn't a trace of anger or resentment in his eyes, though there was a good amount of fear.

Was she that badly hurt?

She checked her other arm, her legs, even patted her chest. When her fingertips went to her forehead, he stopped her. "Don't touch it."

"Is it that bad?"

"Bad enough." He glanced toward the top of the ravine. "Can you get back to the top, with my help?"

"I think so." She managed to sit up by putting her good arm around his shoulders, but standing was impossible. When she tried, the world tilted precariously. The tilting turned to spinning, which caused her to turn her head, afraid she would vomit again.

"Okay. Look. I think you have a concussion, and your arm is…"

"Broken."

"Right. I'm going to have to go for help."

Bethany Yoder was not afraid of the approaching darkness. She wasn't afraid of the ravine either, but suddenly she was very afraid of being alone. She reached for Aaron, clutched his arm, and he moved closer. He let her rest her head against his chest. Without warning, she began sobbing into his shirt.

"Hey, hey, hey. We'll be laughing about this before you know it."

"Ya?"

"Sure. I'll tease you about the time I found you lying in the mud."

"It really h-hur-hurts."

"I'm sure it does. That's why I have to go for help." He kissed her forehead, let his lips linger there. His voice was soft, tender even. "I'll be back in five minutes."

She nodded miserably, and then he was gone.

Bethany sat there in the dark trying to remember what had happened and more than a little grateful that she couldn't. The pain in her arm was unlike anything she'd ever felt before. The angle of her arm had been all wrong, and the swelling had caused it to look hideous… how long had she been down here? Her teeth continued to chatter together, and she realized she was in shock.

She needed to focus, keep herself together until Aaron returned.

But how?

She swiped at the tears running down her cheeks. Her fingers came away red. The blood must be coming from the wound on her head, but Aaron had said not to touch it. She pulled in a very deep, long breath and tried to think of something else, anything else. She felt like a child crying as she sat in the mud. What would Sarah say if she were to see her?

And suddenly, she remembered having a high fever as a child. Sarah had sat by her bed, insisting she take aspirin, bathing her forehead with a cool cloth, checking her temperature again and again. She'd told Bethany that she was a *gut* girl and that she would feel better soon. She'd promised. That promise had helped Bethany to sleep. In the middle of the night, she'd opened her eyes to find her *dat* sitting in Sarah's place. He'd been murmuring a Bible verse over and over. What had it been? Something in Isaiah. She couldn't remember the words exactly, but she thought it had something to do with fear.

Don't be afraid. Gotte is with you.

He will strengthen you.

He will—how did it go?—*He will help you.*

That was it.

He will help you. "He will help me," she whispered. And she realized, in that moment, that *Gotte* already had helped her. He'd sent Aaron.

She saw the beam of flashlights and then heard the voices of Aaron, another man and a woman. The man stood at the top and shone a floodlight down into the ravine. She wasn't sure, but she thought it might be the night watchman her *dat* had recently hired. An older woman and Aaron were making their way back to her.

"This is Maggie. She's staying in site seven. She's a doctor."

"Retired doctor," Maggie corrected. She was slight with short gray hair and a kind smile. "Looks like you took quite the fall, Bethany."

And then suddenly, she remembered what had happened. "I slipped…slipped in the grass as I started down to the creek."

"She was trying to fetch an umbrella," Aaron clarified. "Something I was supposed to do."

"I stumbled, tried to catch myself and felt the bone... um, break, I guess."

"Yes, you definitely have a break there, and a nasty gash on your forehead as well." Maggie opened a first aid kit she'd brought along. "Let's see if we can stop the bleeding first. The ambulance will be here soon."

Ambulance? Was it so bad that she couldn't walk out on her own? Then she remembered how sitting up had caused her to be sick, or perhaps it had been seeing her arm bent at such an unnatural angle.

Maggie had torn open two bandages and placed them on Bethany's forehead, then taped them down.

"Aaron tells me you threw up earlier."

"Yes."

"And you were passed out when he found you?"

"*Ya.* She was." Aaron moved to crouch beside her, a hand on her back, his gaze darting from Bethany to Maggie and back again.

"Do you have a headache?"

"I do."

Maggie tried to shine a penlight into Bethany's eyes, but she jerked away. The light had sent a searing pain through her head.

"Sorry about that." Maggie reached for her right wrist and set two fingers against the inside, smiling as she did so. "Your pulse is good and strong, Bethany, but I suspect you have a concussion."

"What does that mean?"

"It means that you're going to be taking it easy for a few days."

"But the market—"

"The market will be fine without you," Aaron said,

though he added quickly, "It won't be the same, of course, but we'll get along somehow."

"You two are a cute couple," Maggie said.

Bethany had thought she couldn't get any more embarrassed than lying in the mud, her arm swollen and dislocated and apparently a goose egg on her forehead. But she was wrong. She could get more embarrassed.

Aaron didn't seem to notice though.

He reached for her good hand and held it in his.

They all three looked up when they heard the siren.

"Sounds like help has arrived." Maggie stood and waved at the two medical personnel making their way down the slope.

When the paramedics arrived, Maggie updated them on Bethany's condition. One paramedic was a man, and the other a woman, both in their twenties, both cheerful and apparently quite used to this sort of thing. They'd gently placed Bethany's arm that was injured in a padded splint. The pain was still immense, but at least she wouldn't be knocking it against anything.

"I think I can walk."

"Not a chance. Doc Maggie thinks you have a concussion, and I'm agreeing with that assessment." This from the man whose name tag said Grant. "You're riding up, so let us help you onto the stretcher."

Grant carried the front of the stretcher, his back to her, trudging up the embankment as if she weighed nothing at all.

Vicki was the paramedic who had splinted her arm. She cheerfully took the back of the stretcher. Since Bethany was going up the embankment headfirst, she was staring right at Vicki, who smiled and said, "We'll be at the hospital in two shakes of a cat's tail."

Which sounded like something that Ada would say and caused a lump to form in her throat. "My family's going to be worried."

"The night watchman already called the emergency number," Aaron said. "Amos will probably beat us to the hospital."

Her *dat* had a prepaid cell phone for just such emergencies. It didn't have internet, and Bethany couldn't remember it ringing in the last year or more. But her *dat* faithfully charged it every day in his office, then set it on the kitchen counter at home. She'd sort of forgotten about it since she never saw anyone use it.

When they'd carried her out of the creek bed, she was surprised to see what must have been all of the RV guests gathered in a semicircle around the ambulance.

"We're praying for you, Bethany."

"We'll keep Aaron in line while you're gone."

"Just focus on getting well."

As for Aaron, he never left her side, even insisting on climbing into the back of the ambulance with her. Vicki climbed up into the ambulance as well, slapping a blood pressure cuff on her good arm. Grant slammed the back door shut. The last thing Bethany saw outside the door was Maggie waving with one hand, holding on to her first aid kit with the other.

Bethany let her eyes drift to Aaron.

His face was still drained of color, and his eyes were pinned on her as if he were afraid to look away.

"I'll be okay," she said.

He swallowed and nodded. "I know you will be."

She'd said the words to comfort him, but somehow with his hand holding hers and his eyes saying how much she mattered, she believed she would be okay.

She hadn't realized until that moment how difficult it was having him disappointed in her. She hadn't realized until that moment as they rode toward the medical center in the back of an ambulance just how much Aaron King meant to her.

Chapter Ten

❧

"Her arm is broken?"

"*Ya*—between her wrist and her elbow. The doctor thinks it will heal on its own. No surgery, so that's good."

"And a concussion?"

"The knot on her head, it was as big as a tennis ball."

"Wow."

"Exactly."

Aaron and Ethan were sitting in the barn, where they'd always gone to talk—where they'd always gone to escape their father. It was late, close to midnight. It had taken a few hours for the doctors to take X-rays and determine whether Bethany needed surgery. They'd decided to keep her until morning because of the concussion. Her family had been there at that point, surrounding her with exclamations and hugs and even a favorite pillow and the book she'd been reading. Bethany had a *gut* family. Aaron could see that now. It wasn't dysfunctional like his. They didn't mind showing one another that they cared.

He'd watched Amos wipe away tears upon seeing his

doschder laid up in a hospital bed. Amos wasn't embarrassed by his emotions. Instead, he'd stepped forward and enfolded her in his arms, a smile replacing the tears as he assured himself that she was okay.

Aaron wondered what that must have been like—to grow up with a father like that. But for once, he didn't fall into his usual pit of despair. Instead, he was able to acknowledge that her childhood had been different than his, and it was part of what made Bethany who she was. It was one of the reasons that she was so very special to him.

The bishop had insisted on driving Aaron back to pick up his bike at the market and then had also taken him home, strapping the bike on the back of his buggy. Ezekiel hadn't said much; their bishop wasn't one to push or pry. But as he'd driven down Huckleberry Lane, he'd said, "*Gotte* sent you back to us for a reason, Aaron. If not for you, Bethany's condition might have grown far worse. You were a blessing to her, and there will be many people including you in their prayers tonight."

Now, sitting in the barn with Ethan, he tried to wrap his mind around all that had happened in the last six hours.

"It's a *gut* thing that you found her, Aaron. Imagine if she'd lain there all night."

"She shouldn't have been anywhere near that creek. If I'd gone after the umbrella like I was supposed to…"

"I know you think that, but you can't blame yourself for what happened."

"I can blame myself for being a jerk."

"*Ya*. That you can take responsibility for." Ethan reached into the cooler under the workbench and found two sodas, tossed one to him.

Aaron wasn't sure if he needed the caffeine and the sugar, but on the other hand, he might not have the energy to walk inside to his bed if he didn't drink something.

"So, things are *gut* between you two now."

"I guess. I hope so." Aaron popped the top on the soda and took a long drink of the cold sugary beverage. Then he sat there, holding the can between his hands, staring at the lettering—but seeing nothing.

He hesitated, but honestly, he couldn't keep all of his emotions inside himself forever. He needed to start talking to people, especially people he could trust, like his *bruder* and Bethany. "Things seemed better between us. She even let me hold her hand most of the evening, which was a surprise given how mean I'd been to her all day. I overreacted when I figured out that she'd told her family about *dat*'s condition."

"It wasn't like she was gossiping."

"You're right. Turns out she only told them the bare minimum, and she did it because she was worried. Sarah pulled me aside and set me straight on that at the hospital."

"Sarah's a *gut* big *schweschder*."

"That she is."

"She seems a bit protective of her *schweschdern*. I wouldn't mess with her if I were you."

"Ha."

They were silent for a moment. Aaron closed his eyes, grateful for the peace and quiet. It didn't last.

"*Dat* was worse this evening."

Aaron's eyes popped open, and a familiar churning began in his stomach. "What did his doctor say? Did *mamm* tell you?"

"Nothing at all. Because she couldn't. Because he didn't go."

"What?" Now he was wide awake again, and that feeling of peace and quiet—it was entirely gone.

"He refused. Claimed he wasn't feeling well enough to get in the buggy, but then later in the afternoon, he did hitch up Misty."

"Where did he go?"

"I'm not sure, but I suspect back to the library."

"Still wanting us to dig up the crops and plant herbs?"

"*Ya.* He had a lot to say on that subject. Don't worry about that. He is not digging up our crops."

Aaron stood, walked over to the barn's wall and lay his palm flat against it. "Some days, it all seems…too hard."

"It is hard, this thing we're trying to do."

"But maybe it's too hard." Aaron finished the soda and tossed the can into their recycle bin. He walked back to the crate and sat down again, facing his *bruder*. "What if this is all wasted time and energy? You can stop him from pulling up the crops, but we can't watch him every minute. He'll find a new way to destroy whatever we build. He'll lease the land behind our backs or take out another loan or…or…something that we can't even think of."

Ethan didn't answer right away.

Aaron gradually became aware of the night sounds around them—birds calling to one another, a light wind rustling the leaves of the trees, crickets' song.

"What you just said could happen, and you're right that we can't anticipate every way he might bring this down on our heads."

"Then why are we doing it?"

"Because we have to try." Ethan sat forward, elbows on his knees, both hands holding onto his soda can. Finally, he sat up straight, drained what was left of the soda, crushed the can and smiled. "We'll try. We'll do our very best, and if it doesn't work…"

He shrugged, stood and dropped the can into the recycle bin—dropped it next to Aaron's. They were in this together. They'd always been in this together, and Aaron thought that perhaps he hadn't appreciated that enough. He was fortunate to have a *bruder* like Ethan.

"We'll try and do our best and be able to sleep with a clean conscience, because we'll know that we did try."

"Sleep where?"

Ethan slung an arm over Aaron's shoulders as they walked out of the barn and back toward the house. "Can't answer that one because I don't know. The thing is though…we don't have to know the answer to that question. We only have to know what we're going to do tomorrow. I'm going to work in the east field."

"I'm going to work at the market, then go to the Yoders' and check on Bethany."

"See? Sometimes it's like that. You do what you're supposed to do tomorrow and the next day and the day after that."

"Okay."

"Okay?"

"You're saying we need to be satisfied with not having all the answers."

"For now, we'll have to be okay with it. Certainly doesn't do any good to be anxious all day—only makes a person grumpy, and then you're likely to take it out on a friend."

Aaron was too exhausted to argue with Ethan's logic.

Plus, what his *bruder* said had a ring of truth to it. They walked into the house, careful not to wake anyone, undressing in the dark. He was asleep within seconds of his head hitting the pillow, but it wasn't a restful sleep.

His dreams filled with disturbing images, and his heart beat a staccato rhythm.

Ethan's crops had grown head high. Aaron walked through them, searching, growing increasingly desperate. His hands shook and the muscles in his arms began to tremble. Then he was running, first this way, then that, never completely sure of where he was, unable to orient himself to anything familiar. The crops tugged at his clothes as he pushed through them, stopping occasionally to drop to his hands and knees, hoping he would see her.

But he was unable to find Bethany.

He needed to find her. She was in danger, and he needed to help. He stood again, trying to see over the tops of the crop, but the plants had grown even taller. He was unable to see their home. He couldn't find Aaron or his *mamm* or his *dat*. He couldn't find Bethany. His heart pounded harder in his chest, sweat dripped down his face—or was it tears? He reached up to wipe away the wetness, and that's when he saw the storm clouds building on the horizon—towering and black and ominous.

Bethany should have enjoyed the week at home—being waited on, not having to rise early for work, able to lie around and read. But she didn't enjoy it. In fact, she was more than ready to be declared well.

"An apple a day keeps the frowns away," Ada had declared, when she popped out to the front porch with

Bethany's midday snack. Apparently, her *schweschdern* thought if they fed her every few hours, her arm would heal more quickly.

"Tell me about the schoolhouse."

"Well, everything is cleaned up, and the place is closed for the summer." Ada sat back in the rocker, then reached over and snagged one of the apple slices from Bethany's plate.

"And you're sure you don't want to go back?"

"I'm positive. Can you believe *Dat* made me stay the entire year?"

"Actually, I can."

"Well, you know what they say. Teach a woman to fish, and she'll always order pizza."

Bethany had no idea what that meant. Ada was staring at her nails, frowning at them actually.

"Any idea what you want to do next?"

"I don't." She dropped her hands in her lap and tossed a forlorn look at Bethany. "What if I'm not good at anything?"

"Maybe you're not the kind of person who will work outside the home. Maybe, once you're married and having *boppli*, you'll find that was what you were meant to do."

"I don't think so, Bethany. If I don't like a job, I can quit it—well, unless *Dat* says I can't." Her voice dropped lower as she worried a thumbnail. "What if I married and then decided I didn't really love the person? That would be awful. I don't think I know my own mind."

"Hey. You're still very young. Stop putting so much pressure on yourself."

Ada's mood turned sunny. "Some of my friends are going canoeing this afternoon. I know I like that." She popped up, gave Bethany an awkward hug, then hurried into the house.

Bethany loved each of her *schweschdern*, but they all felt particularly protective of Ada. She was the youngest, hadn't known their *mamm* at all and seemed like she was still a child. She wasn't though. She'd recently turned nineteen. She had been out of school many years, and it probably was time that she decided what to do with her life.

That thought made Bethany smile.

It was easier to picture Ada canoeing than it was to picture her settling down. She would, one day—when she found the thing and the person that made her heart happy.

The RV park made Bethany happy. She was surprised how much she missed the little park and the guests and Aaron.

Aaron.

He'd stopped by every afternoon, though it meant riding with her *dat* and then a longer-than-usual bike ride home from their place. He didn't seem to mind. He kept her up to date on the RV park. One guest had brought a cat, and another guest's dog had chased it up onto the roof of their office. He'd had to coax it down with a can of tuna. She could just picture Aaron doing that.

She wanted to be at work. She wanted to be with Aaron.

By the weekend, the pain in her arm had eased up, though the itching had begun. Aaron had brought her one of their s'more metal holders, Sarah had covered the end with batting and fabric, and Bethany carried it with her where ever she went. It fit into her cast perfectly and allowed her to reach the worst of the itching spots.

Sarah had also sewn her a pretty patchwork sling for her arm. It was much better than the one the hospital had given her.

By the next Tuesday she was bound and determined to go back to work.

Her *dat* sipped his morning coffee and frowned. "I don't want you to rush things, Beth. You need to heal."

"I am healed," she assured him. "No headache at all, and *Dat*—there's nothing I can do around here."

She held up her casted arm. "Can't knit or crochet. Can't even clean much. I'm in the way here, and I'd rather be at the market."

He looked as if he were about to ask her something, shook his head once and murmured, "I'm leaving in ten minutes."

She dashed to her room, gathered together her project bag—she couldn't knit, but she could roll skeins of yarn into balls, which were much easier to work with. Checking her reflection in the mirror, she straightened her *kapp*, wondered if she should change dresses and decided it would take too much effort. Putting on a dress and apron was no easy feat when one arm was in a cast. Besides, Aaron wouldn't be looking at her dress. Would he?

She leaned into the small mirror on her wall and addressed her reflection. "You need to slow your roll." It was something she'd heard one of the vendors say the week before. She liked the sound of it, though she knew it wasn't a very Amish thing to say.

She did need to slow down. She was getting ahead of herself. She was thinking about him too much. Just because Aaron had stopped by every day did not mean that he liked her in that way. Did it? He hadn't attempted to kiss her again. If anything, he'd treated her like a basket of eggs. It almost seemed that he was afraid she might break and scatter egg yolk everywhere.

She needed out of this house.

Her analogies were starting to sound like Ada-isms.

The ride to the market was pleasant enough. Her *dat* surprised her when they parked. "After lunch, I'd like you and Aaron to stop by and see me." Then he kissed her on the forehead, making her feel about four years old, and hurried off toward the main office.

Why did he want to see them in his office?

And why hadn't he just told her whatever it was he had to say while they were in the buggy? Obviously, because he wanted Aaron to be there at the same time.

She tossed that around in her mind as she walked across the RV park. Several guests called out to her, and she waved in return. She was surprised when she reached the office to see that Aaron was already there.

He was there and sitting in her chair.

He jumped up as soon as she walked inside.

"Hmmm. Seems a girl can't break her arm and be out for a week without having her chair stolen."

"Bethany. I didn't expect to see you today."

He hurried around the desk and gave her a clumsy hug. "I'll make you some hot tea."

"*Danki*. Tea would be *gut*." She stored her purse in the bottom desk drawer and glanced around. The office looked great. She'd missed it even more than she'd realized. She let out a deep breath and pulled her cat-of-the-day calendar toward her. She tore off every sheet for the last week until she reached May 9. She'd go back and look at the cat pictures later. For now, she wanted to catch up with Aaron.

"How have things been?"

"*Gut*. You mean here? Everything's *gut*. Everyone's asking about you."

"And home?"

"Not so *gut*, to tell you the truth." He set the tea down in front of her, opened a tin of Girl Scout Cookies and put them in the middle of the desk, then plopped in the chair across from her, cradling his mug of coffee. "*Dat*'s worse."

"I'm sorry, Aaron."

He shrugged, sipped his coffee. "Nothing we can do about it at this point. He seems determined to crash again—won't go to the doctor appointments, probably isn't taking his meds."

"But your *mamm*…"

"She watches him, yeah. She tries to be sure he's swallowed them, but if someone is determined not to do a thing, you can't really force him or her."

"Wow."

"What?"

"You seem different is all. Wise all of a sudden."

He pretended to look offended. "And I wasn't wise before?"

"I think you know what I mean."

"*Ya*. I suppose I do." He cleared his throat, reached for three of the cookies and set them on the desk in front of him. "I've realized that I need to stop keeping everything inside."

"That's *gut*."

"It is. I've been talking to my *bruder* more, even sharing my worries with my *mamm*. It's helped, hearing that their concerns reflect my own. We're all doing what we can to help my *dat* be well, but in the end, it's up to him."

"Will you let me know if there's anything we can do to help?"

He finished the cookies, drained the coffee from the mug and stood. Smiling at her, he said, "You already have. You're a *gut* listener, Bethany."

"Danki." Her cheeks felt suddenly warm. She adjusted the homemade sling around her cast. Sarah had used floral fabric in nice spring colors. It cheered Bethany just to look at it.

"How's the gazebo project going?"

"It's a work in progress." He walked across the room and stopped at the door—one hand on the handle, the other in his pocket. "Maybe you can come out to see it later."

"I will."

"After lunch?"

"Okay." Which reminded her... *"Dat* wants to see us."

"He does?"

"After lunch—in his office."

"Ruh-row," he said, and they both laughed. "I can't think of anything I've done wrong. What about you?"

"I haven't even been here."

"True. And he asked to see both of us?"

"He did."

"Then I'll treat you to lunch at the canteen, and we'll both go and see him afterwards."

"Sounds like a deal."

Aaron closed the door. Bethany watched from the window as he walked away, waving a hand in greeting at one of the guests. His attitude had certainly changed since finding her unconscious in the creek.

She wasn't surprised though. She'd always known that there was a less serious, less frightened man underneath the facade that Aaron showed the world. Now if things could just go right for him for a change, perhaps the new Aaron would be the one that she worked with, went to church with and—if her wildest dreams came true—began courting.

Chapter Eleven

The morning sped by for Aaron. He tried to focus on his work, but then he'd remember that Bethany was in the office—Bethany was back! Why was that such a relief to him? He wasn't ready to analyze his feelings, but he was tremendously happy about her return.

He made his way back to the office fifteen minutes early and was surprised to see her sitting on the small front porch, waiting for him. It took all of Aaron's willpower not to reach for Bethany's hand as they walked toward the main portion of the market. They browsed at a few vendor booths and then stopped for lunch at the canteen. After placing.

their orders and retrieving their food, they found a table for two in the corner.

Bethany still had a bump on her forehead, and her arm was in a cast, but otherwise, she seemed like her old self. The bump on her head had gone down, but it was turning a myriad of colors.

"Does it look bad?" She pressed the fingertips of her right hand gingerly against the knot.

"Actually it's turning a lovely shade of purple." He

leaned forward to squint at her forehead. "And yellow and…is that green?"

"Almost makes me wish I were *Englisch* so I could try to cover it up with makeup."

"You don't need makeup. You're beautiful as you are—bruise and all."

She had been about to take a bite of her hot dog, but she stopped with it halfway to her mouth. Setting it back down on her plate, eyes wide and color blazing in her cheeks, she said, *"Danki."*

"Gem gschehne."

Their eyes met, and Aaron wondered if he had a concussion, because suddenly he felt a tad bit dizzy.

Bethany saved the moment from becoming awkward by relating an Ada-ism. "She's decided that a clover a day will keep the doctor away."

"Clover?"

"Yeah, she looks for them everywhere she walks, always manages to find one and brings it to me."

They finished their meal, dumped the trash and walked out into a beautiful May afternoon.

"I didn't realize how tired I was of Sarah's healthy cooking. A hot dog was just what I needed."

"The chips were *gut* too."

"And the brownie. Why did you make me eat a brownie?" She pushed him with her good hand, then laughed when he pretended to stumble.

"It's nice to have you back," he said, his tone suddenly more serious. "It wasn't the same around here without you to give me grief for tracking in mud."

"Ah, yes. Aaron the mud tracker."

"Any idea what your *dat* wants?"

"I can only think of one reason he would need to see us together."

"*Ya*. That's what I thought."

They were a few days shy of their six-week mark. Amos was going to make a decision on which direction the RV park would go, and Aaron had no idea what he hoped the man would say. He still thought he was right, but he also understood what benefits Bethany's plan brought to the equation.

"Hard to believe it's been six weeks since you tracked mud across my newly hooked rug."

"The time has flown." He held the door for her, and they made their way to Amos's office.

Amos looked up and smiled when they tapped on his doorframe. The door itself was always open. He believed in being accessible to his employees.

"Right on time. Come in." He waited until they'd settled in the chairs across from him. "I guess you both know why you're here."

Aaron nodded, as did Bethany.

"I was going to wait until Beth came back to work next week, but since she insisted on returning a week earlier than the doctor suggested…" He spread out his hands. "Might as well get it over with."

"Sounds foreboding." Bethany aimed for light, but the look she sent Aaron proved she was worried.

"To review…" He pulled a folder toward him.

By now, Aaron understood that Amos had a folder for everything. The man was seriously organized. He supposed you had to be in order to efficiently run a place this size.

"Bethany, you wanted the RV park to have a Plain and simple tone."

"*Ya*, I did, but the ideas Aaron had, they've been *gut* too. The firepit has been a big success, and the horseshoe area and washer pit—well, it seems as if there are always guests there."

Amos raised an eyebrow, but he didn't comment on that. "Aaron, you envisioned more of a plain and simple *resort*—a place with amenities that would set us apart from other RV parks."

"Sure, and I stand by those ideas, but Bethany…well, what she does with the guests really works. The cookies make them smile, and the handmade items are always a big hit. She helps them to feel at home."

Amos closed the folder and steepled his fingers together. "It seems to me as if you've both learned how to appreciate what each other brings to the table."

Aaron nodded, then glanced at Bethany, who was nodding too. They looked like two bobbleheads sitting there nodding at her father.

"I happen to agree. I've received feedback from the people who have camped here in the last few weeks, and they mention both the new amenities as well as the homemade touches. They gave us five-star ratings and noted that they plan to return."

Now he smiled, dropped his hands and leaned back in his chair. "I've made my decision. I'm going to use both of your plans. We're going to merge them into one fine RV establishment."

"It's a *wunderbaar* idea," Aaron said.

"I love it," Bethany added.

"We're not out of the woods yet. I need you to stay above a ninety percent occupancy rate. I need customers to remain happy and recommend us to their friends. If both of those things happen—and I fully expect they will, then I think we can make the RV park a permanent part of our market."

Aaron high-fived Bethany.

"Before you both celebrate too grandly, there's still plenty of work to do. I'm formally making you both directors of the RV park. Aaron, I'm going to assign a helper to you so that you can finish the gazebo. Bethany, I want a supply order from you of things that you can embellish in a simple way…" He grinned again at his use of the word *simple*. "Let's keep those welcome and come-back-soon packages going. Let's make them better than ever."

"Sure thing."

Aaron and Bethany walked to the door, but Aaron needed to say something else to Amos. He snagged Bethany's arm. "I'll catch up with you. Okay?"

"Sure."

She smiled at him, then turned and continued down the hall. Aaron walked back into the office, thanked Amos and shook his hand. "I appreciate your giving me an opportunity to work here, taking a chance on me."

"It wasn't much of a chance…your family has always been well liked, and you and Ethan are obviously hard workers."

"But my *dat*…"

"What your *dat* does and doesn't do is on him. You make your own reputation, Aaron. You've made a *gut* one. I'm not the only person who thinks so."

Aaron wasn't sure how to respond to Amos's words, so he thanked him again and hurried to catch up with Bethany.

He was relieved, of course, but he'd never had what he thought of as his father's blessing. He'd never been told, "Well done, son." He'd certainly never been told that he made someone proud, though his *mamm* had complimented him from time to time. Not often. Most days, her plate was completely full taking care of his *dat*. What had that been like for her? How did she keep at it day after day and year after year?

He vowed to thank her that evening for all that she did. Everyone could use a little appreciation. He'd been too self-absorbed for too long to realize that.

When he walked back out into the sunshine, Bethany was waiting for him. He couldn't believe how different today felt from that first day six weeks ago. As they walked back to the RV park, other employees called out to him and Bethany, raising a hand in greeting and telling Bethany it was grand to have her back.

It seemed to Aaron that his life was beginning to make sense. He could do this. He could be good at this.

The only question, the only thing holding him back, was the status of things at home. His mind flashed back on his dream that had repeated itself more than once in the last week. He pushed the images away. There was nothing he could do about coming storms.

He'd discussed his father's downward spiral with Ethan, with his *mamm* and with Bethany. It seemed that the only thing he could do was wait and stay out of the way of the tempest that would surely come.

He would continue working to the best of his ability today. Tomorrow would have to take care of itself.

Tomorrow, he would have to leave in the Lord's hands.

The next ten days passed like a whirlwind for Bethany. Her arm continued to heal. The bruise on her forehead turned from purple to a light green and then a pale yellow.

"You're a duck of a different color now," Ada had declared.

May in Northern Indiana was a thing of beauty. The days were warm, the nights cool and the rains moved through quickly. Pink, yellow and purple wildflowers bloomed everywhere, and the vegetable gardens that had been planted a month before were growing lush. Some of the crops were waist-high. It felt like a time of abundance and blessings. It felt like a good life.

Market days were busy, the crowds always seeming to surpass the previous day's numbers. As for the RV park, they'd had to start turning people away. Aaron was putting the finishing touches on the gazebo, and the dog park was a big hit. Gideon had helped set the fence posts into concrete. They'd also added two benches for dog owners to sit on, as well as a poop bag dispenser and a large trash can. Aaron had even thought to construct a few playthings for the pups.

A piece of plyboard cut in half vertically and positioned together like a teepee made for a nice climbing toy. He'd supported it with poles and nailed cross boards so that the dogs could stand at the top, paws braced against the boards and survey their domain. Round bar stools that had been thrown away by the local ice cream shop became stepping paws. Aaron had given them a bright coat of paint and cut the supporting pole down to somewhere between one and two feet. Bethany always laughed when she looked over and saw dogs sitting on them.

Things at the RV park were going great.

One surprise that floored Bethany was that she was

asked out by two different guys who had never shown any interest in her previously.

"Do you think I was asked out because of pity?" she'd asked Becca. "Like, because of my bruise and arm they feel sorry for me?"

She was standing in the doorway to Becca and Gideon's room. Gideon was outside helping her *dat* and Eunice. They were working on a water trough. The pump had gone out, causing the trough to overflow. Water and mud were everywhere.

Becca patted the place beside her on the bed. "Sit. Let's talk."

"That sounds serious."

"We don't have private conversations often enough, and some things...well, some things are hard to discuss at the dinner table."

Becca was only five years older, but it seemed to Bethany that their age difference had increased in the last year. Bethany still felt like a *youngie*. Becca, on the other hand, now seemed like a woman.

"You've changed," Bethany said as she took her place on the bed.

Becca had scooted back so that she was leaning against the headboard.

"Don't look surprised. It's true. You're all grown up now. Clearly, you've left me and Eunice and Ada in the dust. It's like you're...well, more woman than girl."

Becca glanced out the window, but she didn't speak right away.

"Is it being married, or is it...what you did before?"

"You mean the mission work?" Now Becca's attention was fully on Bethany. "I'd say it's both, but maybe not in the way you think. It's hard to explain."

"Try, because I'd really like to know."

Becca nodded, pulled her *kapp* strings to the front and studied them a moment. "Being away helped me to see our life here differently, and assisting people whose lives were destroyed by floods or fire or tornadoes… well, that helped me appreciate all we have."

"Maybe we all should serve on a mission trip."

Becca smiled. "Being married changes you too."

"How?" She was really interested. She'd thought about marrying, of course she had. Most Amish women did marry. In fact, she was quickly becoming one of the few people her age unmarried. "You and Gideon, you're the first married couple I've seen up close. I don't remember *Mamm* as well as you do. It's been the five of us and *Dat* for all of my life."

"True."

"Is marriage all you thought it would be? You seem happy."

"I am happy." Becca's expression remained serious, but the look in her eyes softened. "But it's not all butterflies in your stomach and stolen kisses."

"Surely, there's some of that."

"There is." Becca smiled and looked out the window again. "For me, marriage has been about my world becoming bigger, learning to care about someone else as much as I care about myself, laughing when they laugh and hurting when they hurt."

"Is Gideon hurting?"

"He's worried about his *bruder*. Luke isn't adjusting as well as we'd hoped."

"I'm sorry."

"Plus, Nathan's health is a little worse. He'll probably be moving soon."

"Oh." Luke was living with Nathan. If Nathan was moving, Luke would have to move too. Would he go back to Texas? Or would he move in with them? That didn't seem possible. Where would he sleep? She thought of the illustrated book she'd read as a child. *There was an old woman who lived in a shoe…*

Becca blew out a breath, then smiled. "Let's talk about you."

"Me?" Bethany's voice squeaked, and she brought it down to a normal level. "I'm fine. Healing up great." She raised her cast. "See?"

"Samuel Mast asked you out?"

"He did."

"And James Lapp?"

"How do you know?"

"Gideon works at the market, Bethany. He's the assistant manager. He hears things."

"Yikes."

"He didn't hear anything bad. Both Samuel and James were disappointed that you said no."

"Huh."

"Why did you say no?"

"Well, James is too young."

"He's your age."

"Seems younger."

"And Samuel?"

"He's a nice guy, but I just don't feel…any butterflies."

"Ah."

Bethany rather regretted walking into her *schweschder*'s room. She would much rather ignore her feelings than analyze them.

"It's okay to say no. I'm not judging you. No one in this house is judging you."

"But—"

"But it's also okay to say yes."

"You lost me."

Becca cleared her throat, then reached for Bethany's good hand and squeezed it. "You're waiting for Aaron, right? Waiting for him to want to start dating? Waiting for him to ask you out?"

"I don't know." Had her feelings been so obvious? She'd thought she was doing a good job of keeping them to herself, of keeping them hidden. "I don't know what I'm doing. I've never felt this way before."

"*Ya*. Love is like that sometimes."

"I didn't say I was in love."

"Are you?"

"Maybe." And somehow saying it felt right. It felt like she was finally giving voice to what was growing in her heart. "His family situation, well, it breaks my heart. And I think that he's afraid to commit, afraid to even allow himself to feel anything because he can't say what tomorrow will be like."

"But that's true for all of us."

"I guess."

"Look." Becca stood, then pulled Bethany to her feet, marched her into the bathroom and turned them both toward the mirror. "You are a beautiful person— inside and out. It's okay for you to want to explore your feelings with Aaron. It's okay to wait, but, honey, you can't wait forever. Aaron's family situation might not ever resolve."

"Then what do I do?"

"Pray for him."

"I do."

"Give him the space and time he needs."

"I'm trying."

"Maybe ask him out."

Bethany turned from her reflection, turned to look directly at Becca. "Seriously?"

"Sure. We are, after all, modern women."

"Modern Amish women."

"Yup."

"I hadn't even considered asking him out."

"Give it some thought. And if he says no, maybe give James or Samuel a chance."

"Why would I do that?"

"Well, it doesn't hurt to see what else is out there." Becca winked at her, gave her a final hug, then went to the kitchen to help Sarah with dinner.

Bethany just stood there, wondering if she had the courage to do what Becca had suggested. She stared at her reflection in the small mirror. She was only twenty years old, but she felt as if her life were sand slipping through an hourglass.

She decided she needed fresh air, needed a walk to clear her head, and of course, she ended up at the fence feeding carrot pieces to Oreo and Peanut and Kit Kat. She could see her *dat* and Gideon and Eunice working in the adjacent pasture, but she stayed where she was. She stayed with the horses.

She thought back over what Becca had said, trying to put a finger on what had bothered her. It was like probing for a hurt tooth with your tongue, trying to figure out exactly which one was causing the pain.

She was waiting on Aaron.

Was she?

Yes. She definitely was. She could be honest with herself.

She was waiting to see what he'd do next, if he'd make the next move.

And though things between them had been better—much better—he hadn't kissed her again. If anything, he seemed to be going out of his way to make sure they spent little or no time alone. Why was that?

Was he afraid of getting closer?

Or had he changed the way that he thought of her? Was she becoming more of a *schweschder* or best friend and less of a love interest? Had she imagined that he had deeper feelings for her?

The questions piled up until she felt as if she might topple over into the field because of the weight of them.

They were all good questions.

She could keep wondering, keep waiting, or…

Maybe, it was time that she asked him.

Chapter Twelve

Aaron went to bed with a raging headache.

His *dat* had grown increasingly irritated throughout the night. He began lecturing them at dinner about his idea to switch to growing herbs, moved on to his doctors' incompetency and ended with the familiar mantra that everyone was against him. Aaron, Ethan and his *mamm* fled to the front porch for a family conference.

"He's worse," Ethan said.

"He's spiraling down." Aaron hated saying it, hated the look of resignation on his *mamm*'s face, but now wasn't the time for denial.

She pulled in a deep breath and squared her shoulders. "We'll call the bishop in the morning, ask him to come out and collect your *dat*, ask him to take your *dat* back to the center in Middlebury."

"It's the best thing," Ethan said.

Aaron didn't know what to say, so he trudged off to look after the horses. Ethan joined him in the barn, and they worked an hour, doing any little thing that needed to be done, trying to give their father time to wind down or at least fall asleep.

It didn't happen.

They'd finally trudged inside at ten o'clock only to hear the sound of voices arguing in the kitchen. To be more exact, his *dat*'s voice was loud and argumentative. His *mamm*'s voice, as always, was calm and compassionate.

"You should come to bed," Esther said.

"I already told you that I'm not tired. Why do you keep bothering me?"

"Zackary, you need to take your meds, and then you need to come to bed."

"I'm not taking that poison."

His father's voice had taken on a dangerous tone, a growl almost. Both Ethan and Aaron moved toward the kitchen, ready to intercede if necessary. They stopped at the doorway and were met by an all-too-familiar scene.

"Is everything okay in here?" Ethan asked.

"Just dandy, other than the fact that your *mamm* and that crazy doctor are trying to kill me." Zackary was sitting at the table. He tried to look at them defiantly— hair askew, eyes wide but red from lack of sleep, gaze jerking from one thing to another. He couldn't quite hold the rebellious posture. His elbows propped on the table, he dropped his head into his hands.

Their *mamm* attempted to touch his shoulder, but Zackary jerked away. She closed her eyes a moment, as if to utter a time-worn prayer, then slipped from the room.

Aaron realized in that moment that his father had shrunk. People did that as they grew older. Or perhaps it was more that the effects of his illness had worn him down. He looked slighter, older and confused. Aaron felt a moment of sympathy for the man.

But then Zackary sat up straighter, brought his hand

down hard on the table and raised his voice. "Can't you just leave me alone?"

Reluctantly, they did.

They left him there.

Aaron looked back to see that his *dat* had once again let his head drop into his hands. He was sitting there alone, trying to stand up to the confusion in his mind. An oil lamp sat on the table. Nothing else—not a cup of coffee or plate of cookies. Nothing to explain why he remained there.

By the time Aaron had washed up and crawled into bed, his head was aching. He should go into the kitchen and find some aspirin, but he couldn't face another confrontation. Instead, he closed his eyes, focused on his breathing, and soon he was asleep.

The dream was the same but also different.

He was once again walking through crops that were head high. He was searching like all the previous times, but this time his desperation was more pronounced, more frightening. His heart beat faster than it should. He could hear his pulse thundering in his ears. Sweat poured down his face, his back, under his arms. His breath came out in ragged gasps.

He continued walking and frantically looking to his left and right, though he couldn't have said for what. Like every time before, he began running. He was lost, afraid, desperate. His clothes caught on the crops, tearing as he pushed through ears of corn, stalks of hay and barley.

He needed to find his *mamm*. He needed to get to her.

He looked up, knowing even as he did that he would once again see the dark storm clouds, but this time he didn't. This time he saw smoke—black, thick and filling the horizon. He stared at it a moment, utterly dumbfounded. Then he covered his mouth with the sleeve of his shirt, and he began to run.

Aaron hit the floor with a thud.

The dream. He'd had the dream again. He coughed, tried to open his eyes and coughed some more—great hacking sounds that hurt his chest, and then he realized that his eyes were burning.

The fire.

The fire in his dream.

He sat up on the floor, but he saw only darkness.

Then he noticed it—a red glow barely visible under the door. He jerked open his bedroom door and saw that the hallway was filled with smoke. He sprinted toward the glow of the fire, ran for the kitchen.

Ethan was already there, pulling their *dat* from the room. "Get *Mamm* outside."

Aaron turned and ran for his parents' room. Esther had opened the door and was tying the sash around her night-robe. Her eyes widened as she realized what was happening.

"Zackary…"

"He's outside. Ethan has him. We have to go, *Mamm*."

"But—"

"We have to go." He pulled her across the living room, prepared to carry her if he had to, but Esther King was no fool. She understood that it would be reckless to try and save any of their things. And what would she choose? The Bible beside her bed? The box filled with her sons' school papers? The letters from family? Aaron could practically see the thoughts cross her mind and quickly disappear.

"All right." She nodded and quickened her step.

The kitchen was now completely engulfed in fire, and the flames were creeping toward the living area.

They stumbled out into the yard, and Aaron's gaze went straight to the barn. Though it was old, worn and its roof leaked, it stood like a beacon in a terrible night. The barn was fine. Misty was fine, and they still had the crops.

But the house—the house was in flames.

By the time they retreated to the far part of the yard, the fire department was pulling down Huckleberry Lane—several trucks and at least a dozen volunteer firefighters. They fanned out around the house, calling to one another in a way that assured Aaron they had done this before. It was just another night on the job for them. It was nothing they couldn't handle.

Apparently, a neighbor had called in the blaze.

Aaron, Ethan, Zackary and Esther were moved farther from the house. A police car arrived. More neighbors showed up—Amish and *Englisch*. Someone passed around paper cups filled with coffee from a thermos. Someone else wrapped a blanket around Esther.

The bishop arrived, and after him, more members of their church began pulling into their farm. Aaron glanced over to see Amos Yoder and Ben Lapp speaking to Ezekiel. He waited and watched. Ezekiel looked up, met Aaron's gaze, then nodded in agreement to something that Ben said.

Gideon approached the family. "Are you sure everyone's okay?"

"Yes, the paramedics already checked us out. I'd like to speak with you—privately." Ethan cleared his throat and looked at Aaron. "Can you stay here with *Mamm*?"

"Of course."

Ethan motioned for Gideon to step away with him.

Aaron made out a few words—*our dat…hospital… not well.*

Gideon listened intently, put a hand on Ethan's shoulder, then went to speak with one of the police officers. Ethan returned to the small family group, nodding at Aaron as if they had agreed on something.

A large burly man with Fire Chief stenciled on his protective coat finally approached his parents. "The fire itself was contained to the kitchen and a small portion of the living room, but I'm afraid the smoke damage is quite extensive."

Esther nodded as if that made sense. "Is it safe for us to go back inside now?"

The fire chief didn't even hesitate. "No. It's not. Neither the kitchen nor the house is accessible at this point. We're still watching for hot spots. In a few hours, we can let you go in and get some clothing and personal items."

"Why would we—"

"*Mamm*, we can't stay here." Ethan crossed his arms, stared at their home and then put a hand on his mother's arm. "I've spoken with Gideon, who explained the situation to Bishop Ezekiel. The police officer will take *Dat* to Middlebury. Ben and Martha Lapp have offered to take you in."

"Take me in?"

"Let you stay with them. Until we can assess the damage and schedule a workday."

"Is that really necessary? For us to leave?"

"It is, ma'am." The fire chief shouted something to a driver of one of the pump trucks, then turned back to Esther. "At this point, your home isn't fit to stay in.

Once we're sure the fire is out, you'll have to clean away the debris and rebuild. Wouldn't want the roof coming down on your heads." Then he rushed off to speak to firefighters who were spraying water around the barn.

"All right, but what about you boys?"

"We'll stay with Amos."

"For how long?"

"As long as necessary."

Aaron barely took in what Ethan said. One part of his mind understood. His *mamm* would stay with the Lapps. They would stay with the Yoders. He heard all of those details, but they weren't registering yet, because he was watching his father. He'd looked alternately confused and terrified. Now he covered his face with his hands and began to weep—giant wracking sobs that caused Aaron's throat to ache.

"I'm sorry. I'm so very sorry."

And Aaron believed that he was, but his *dat*'s remorse didn't solve a thing. He'd finally done it. He'd finally managed to cross a line that couldn't be uncrossed. They could repair the house. They could probably move back in before the end of the month, but they'd never again be safe with their *dat*.

Sarah shook Bethany awake.

"What is it? What's wrong?" She sat up blinking and trying to force her eyes to focus.

"There's been a fire at Aaron's house."

Bethany must have attempted to vault out of the bed, but Sarah's hand stayed her. "Everyone is fine. The fire is nearly out."

She glanced over at Ada's bed. The covers were thrown back and Ada was gone. Was everyone up except for her?

A glance toward the window showed the sun hadn't yet begun to rise.

"How much of the house was damaged?"

"I don't have any additional details, but Bishop Ezekiel called *Dat*'s emergency phone. Ethan and Aaron will be staying here with us until their home is repaired. I'm going to start breakfast."

Bethany searched Sarah's face for any indication that she might be holding something back. She wasn't. Sarah wouldn't do that. Her *schweschder* was telling her everything that she knew. Bethany had the horrible feeling of being caught in a nightmare; only this wasn't a dream. This was actually happening.

"They'll be hungry and tired. Eunice has gone to the barn to clean out a stall for their mare. We'll bed her there until she gets used to the place. Becca will help me in the kitchen. I need you and Ada to move Eunice's and my things into here."

"Here?"

"We can't put Aaron and Ethan in the living room. They'll need a bit of privacy."

"All four of us are going to be in here?"

She looked around the small room. There were two twin beds, a night table, hooks on the wall for dresses, cubbies built beneath the hooks to hold their things and a reading chair. "What will you sleep on?"

"We'll make up two pallets on the floor. There are sleeping bags and mattress pads in the mudroom."

"Wow."

"It'll be just like old times when we used to camp out at the pond."

Bethany hadn't thought of that in years. The shock and grief momentarily lifted, and then crashed back on her as she remembered what was happening. Aaron's house had caught on fire? Tears filled her eyes, and a few slipped down her cheeks.

Sarah pulled her into a hug, squeezed gently and then stood. "Chop chop. Lots to do."

And wasn't that Sarah's way? A moment of compassion and then on to what must be done.

Bethany threw on her housecleaning dress, then splashed water on her face and combed her hair. She affixed her older *kapp* with bobby pins, then hurried out into the hall. Ada was already moving Sarah's and Eunice's clothes.

"I'm sure they're fine, Bethany."

"You can't know that."

"They're coming here, not the hospital." Ada tossed her a reassuring smile. "We're going to be packed in tighter than carrots in a can."

"Sardines," Bethany murmured, but Ada's quip made her smile. The world might have turned topsy-turvy, but her family remained the same.

They spent the next hour moving all of Sarah's and Eunice's things into their room. Bethany hurried to the mudroom and found the sleeping bags and pads. The sleeping bags needed a good airing, so she unzipped them and hung them across the porch railing. Looking to the east, she was surprised to see the faintest glow of a May sunrise.

She paused for a moment, murmured a prayer of thanksgiving that no one had been hurt, then rushed back inside to sweep the floor in their bedroom. Ada was attempting to pull the reading chair out of their room. Bethany leaned the broom against the wall and helped her. They put the chair into Gideon and Becca's room. It fit, though just barely.

They positioned the pads—one between their beds and the other across the end.

"We can tiptoe through if we're careful." Ada actually clapped her hands. "It'll be just like a slumber party."

"Let's find some extra sheets and quilts." They did and left them folded on the end of the pads. "We'll make them up after the sleeping bags have had a good airing."

"Good thing we both sleep with two pillows." Ada tossed one of hers onto the pad between their beds.

Bethany set hers down on the pad at the end of their beds.

Was she thinking their home was crowded before? It was about to be much more so. She thought of Aaron sleeping down the hall from her. How awkward would that be? It didn't matter. She'd deal with those emotions later.

As Bethany and Ada walked into the kitchen to help with breakfast, they heard the clatter of buggy wheels. All five girls crowded in at the window, and that closeness more than anything else eased the worry in Bethany's mind.

As they watched, Gideon pulled in, Kit Kat tossing her head and looking happy about the early morning trip. Her *dat* hopped out of the buggy and stood there waiting for Aaron and Ethan. Another buggy joined the first, the older horse doing its job, but looking as if she might sleep on her feet.

"I wonder where Esther went," Eunice murmured.

"And Zackary?" Becca's voice was pensive.

They didn't know the details yet, but one look told

Bethany that they were thinking the same thing. They all suspected Aaron's *dat* had something to do with the fire. If so, what did that mean? Would he be back at the hospital or in the town's small jail?

Ada began putting plates on the table.

Becca pulled out coffee mugs.

Sarah turned to the stove to check on the breakfast casserole and hot bread.

Eunice went out the back door to see if she could help with the horses.

And Bethany? Bethany couldn't have stopped herself if she'd tried. She followed Eunice out the door, ran down the porch steps and threw herself into Aaron's arms. For the briefest of moments, he wrapped his arms around her, and finally—finally the ache she'd felt since being shook awake eased.

The moment didn't last.

Aaron dropped his arms, took a step back from her, and when he spoke, he wouldn't quite meet her eyes.

"We're okay," Aaron said, his voice trembling with emotion.

"Everyone? Your *mamm* and *dat*?"

"*Ya.* No one was injured in the fire." He took another step back, crossing his arms and hunching his shoulders as if to ward off the cold…but it wasn't cold. The things he was unconsciously trying to protect himself against had nothing to do with the weather. He glanced toward the barn. "I should go and help."

"Okay. *Ya.* Of course." She swiped at the tears that had streamed down her face—a little embarrassed but mostly just relieved. "Okay."

She walked back to the house slowly, trying to figure out what had just happened. He'd plainly been relieved to see her. She hadn't imagined his arms holding her close, and then... What had happened then?

Twenty minutes later, they were all gathered around the breakfast table. They usually bowed their heads for a silent prayer before eating, but everything about today was different. Wordlessly, Amos reached for Sarah's hand. Sarah reached for Becca's. Around the table, this circle of grace was knit until they were one.

Her *dat*'s voice was low, filled with reverence and gratitude. "Father, we thank you for your mercy and your grace. We thank you for watching over Ethan and Aaron, for sparing their lives and the lives of their parents. For sparing much of their home, the barn, the mare, the crops. I thank you for the opportunity for my family to show grace and kindness to Ethan and Aaron with the certain knowledge that they would do the same in our hour of need. Watch over us, guide us, strengthen us."

The *amens* echoed around the table, and it reminded Bethany of the sound of a gentle rain on the roof. Then she realized it was raining. When had that started? The last she remembered was seeing a bit of the sunrise toward the east. But that had been hours ago.

"The rain is good, *ya*? It'll put out any hot spots, for sure and certain." Gideon took a giant helping of egg, ham and cheese and passed the casserole dish to his right.

There was such abundance here.

Bethany had never seen it before. She'd never noticed.

But now, realizing that the Kings had lost so much, Bethany was painfully aware of all that they had—the food, the table, the roof over their heads. Perhaps this was what Becca had felt when she'd gone on her mission trips, when she'd helped those who had nothing left due to no fault of their own.

Gratitude.

Overwhelming gratitude.

The details of the night washed over her as she ate. Ethan did all of the talking. Their *dat* had plummeted from his manic phase to a depressed one. He'd been up late. Probably he'd fallen asleep at the kitchen table and knocked over the lantern. The fire had gutted the room, the rest of the house was intact, but there was plenty of smoke damage. A workday would be scheduled soon. The benevolence fund would cover the expense.

After the meal, after Aaron and Ethan had cleaned up, when her family was going their different directions—because it was, after all, still a workday—Bethany stood on the front porch with Aaron. The rain had slowed to a drip, and it looked as if the sun would peek through soon.

They hadn't had a moment alone, and now Bethany wasn't sure exactly what to say. Maybe she didn't need to say anything. Maybe she needed to give him time to sort through his emotions.

He turned toward her, crossed his arms and rested his backside against the porch railing. His eyes were on her, and Bethany was thinking of how it had felt to stand within the circle of his arms. She was thinking of how natural it had been to go to him, to try to comfort him, to be comforted by him.

She didn't do that now though.

Everything about his body language said, *Please stay away.*

She sat in one of the rockers, facing him, waiting.

"Ethan and I appreciate this, more than you can know."

"It's what neighbors do, Aaron. We're glad you're here."

He raised an eyebrow, obviously doubtful. "Four of you in a single room? You should have put us up in the barn."

"Ada's quite excited about it. She says it will be like a slumber party."

"Can't say as I've ever been to one of those."

"They usually involve loads of talking, snacking and laughing...very little sleep. Sarah will put up with it for about an hour."

Aaron smiled, the first real smile she'd seen from him that day.

"What will happen to your *dat*?"

"Bishop Ezekiel arranged for a driver to take him and my *mamm* to the medical center in Middlebury. He'll stay there for a while. *Mamm* will stay with Ben and Martha Lapp."

He sighed, and such pain crossed his face that Bethany felt as if she were pierced by it.

"I am so, so sorry. That sounds...really...insufficient, but I am."

"Actually, it's kind." He scrubbed his hands over his face, then moved to the rocker beside her. "We had decided last night—before the fire—that we would take my *dat* back today. He was out of control, but we never thought...we never thought this would happen. We never thought one more night would make a difference."

"You couldn't have known."

"Maybe. Or maybe we should have known."

"Everything's been going so well—at the market, I mean. You've really found your place there."

"And Ethan's done a great job with the crops, but this is the way it is…" He turned to look at her fully now. "This is the way it is with my *dat*. It's always one step forward and two steps back. It's always progress, but progress in the wrong direction."

"Maybe this time—"

He held up a hand to stop her. "I don't believe that anymore."

She didn't know what to say to that. Perhaps he was simply tired. Maybe he'd be more optimistic after a good night's rest, after the rebuilding began, after he was back in his own home.

He stood and so did she.

He stepped closer.

She stepped closer.

He put his hands on her shoulders and looked at her directly.

She thought maybe he'd kiss her.

He didn't. He waited until he had her complete attention. "I hope you can see now why we can't be a couple. Whatever we're feeling…it's hopeless. It's a fool's dream."

"I don't believe that."

"But I do, and it takes two to make a relationship work. I can't. I won't."

"Can't and won't what?" His words were making her throat hurt, making her heart ache.

"I can't be that selfish, Bethany. I won't put you through what I live through every day." He tucked a lock of hair into her *kapp*. "You deserve better."

And then he was gone, striding across to the barn and disappearing inside.

Chapter Thirteen

The next ten days, Aaron felt as if he were walking underwater—as if he were viewing the real world, the one where everyone else lived, from a distance. At work, he kept his head down and focused on his tasks. He stopped going to the office unless he knew Bethany wasn't there. He took to leaving her notes if there was anything he needed to communicate. Those notes were always brief and to the point.

At the Yoders' farm, it was a bit more difficult to avoid people. With nine adults living under the same roof, it was rare that he found time or space to be alone. That didn't stop him from trying. He'd tackle the worst chore if it meant that he could do it by himself.

Even at church, he felt as if he were both there and not there.

He couldn't have explained why he was avoiding any contact with others. It simply felt as if his skin, but more than likely his emotions, had been chaffed by the fire. It simply hurt too much to be around people. Participating in any sort of conversation required more of him than he had to give.

He managed to at least mumble a thanks to all of the people who offered condolences regarding the fire. When they asked what they could do to help, he plastered on a smile that felt like a grimace and said, "I think it's all covered."

It wasn't.

That was painfully obvious to him, but he could not be that blatantly honest with these people. He could see that they were genuinely trying to be kind, to be helpful, but he couldn't reach across the great expanse that separated his life from all others. That seemed too difficult. That seemed impossible.

Ethan drove the buggy back to their home on Huckleberry Lane every day. He seemed almost unfazed by what had happened. Like before the fire, he worked hard in the fields all day, came home exhausted at night and fell asleep as soon as he laid down in the evening.

They spoke to their *mamm* from the closest phone booth every other night. She seemed to be doing well. She let them know how sorry their father was about the fire, what the doctors were doing to help stabilize him, how kind the Lapps were to put her up as long as was needed. She always ended those phone calls with "Keep the faith," but Aaron had no idea what that meant.

Work was busier than ever, and by the time Aaron arrived back at Bethany's house at the end of each day, he should have been exhausted. Instead, he was filled with a restless energy. He took long, solitary walks around their property and went out of his way to avoid being alone with Bethany. The hurt in her eyes on that first morning they'd been there, when he'd explained to her why they couldn't pursue a relationship—well, that had been every bit as painful to him as seeing his family's home go up in flames.

He had caused her enough pain. He absolutely refused to cause her any more.

Unfortunately, simply avoiding Bethany wasn't quite resulting in the isolated life he felt he needed and deserved.

Sarah insisted on making huge lunches for him and Ethan to take with them. Eunice wanted to talk to him about how they could upgrade things at the RV park using solar energy. He could gruffly thank Sarah and brush off Eunice, but he couldn't hold back a smile when Ada told him, "Nose up! Tomorrow's another day."

"She means 'chin up'..." Sarah shook her head, but smiled tenderly at her younger *schweschder*.

Being around Amos wasn't any easier than spending time with the rest of the family. He was the same man at home that he was at the market—calm, willing to listen, only offering his opinion if you asked for it. Being around Amos made Aaron ache for what his life might have been like—if he'd had a normal father, if his *dat* had even once put their needs over his own impulses, if he were a better son who could accept things as they were.

But it was being around Gideon and Becca that caused Aaron the most pain. Their love was still so young. They were only a few years older than him and Bethany. Their lives weren't perfect. Gideon was still trying to figure out the best way to help his *bruder*. It was also obvious that he cared for Nathan and that the old guy's upcoming move was worrying him. And he and Becca still didn't have their own home, though they'd begun making plans for where they would build it on Amos's property.

Gideon's life was as different and unattainable as moving to the moon.

Gideon would someday soon have a new home. He had a new bride. Within a year, maybe two, he'd have a *boppli*. He was living the idyllic Amish life. Aaron didn't resent that, but he couldn't help thinking that he would never have the things that Gideon did. His life was an impending train wreck, and he could not find a way to hop off before he was crushed in the collision.

For Memorial Day week, the market was open Monday through Wednesday. They had the biggest crowds that Aaron had seen to date. The RV park was completely full, and he was helping in the market whenever he wasn't needed at the RV Park. By the time he was back at the Yoder place on Wednesday evening and had enjoyed another delicious dinner by Sarah that he could barely remember wolfing down, he was too tired to take his normal evening walk, which allowed him to avoid everyone. He headed to the back side of the barn instead. Misty could use a good currying, and doing it properly would take at least an hour. Hopefully by then, everyone would have scattered to their rooms.

He simply could not abide an hour of family time, though as he picked up the grooming brush, he could easily imagine what they were all doing. Eunice was probably beating Sarah at chess again. Becca and Gideon were sitting side by side on the couch, looking through some type of catalog and no doubt holding hands. Ada could break into any conversation with a misquoted quip, and Amos would be reading *The*

Budget—same edition of the paper he'd read the night before.

As for his *bruder*, Ethan, he fit in with that group like a well-worn glove fit on your hand. He'd encourage Sarah that she might win this time, laugh at Ada's quips and ask Bethany about the RV park. Ethan seemed able to live in the moment in a way that Aaron envied but couldn't quite achieve.

Then there was Bethany, always pretending to work on some bit of needlework though her arm was still in a cast. She continually threw glances his way as if waiting for him to take back the words he'd said.

Nope.

He was better off with the mare.

He'd been brushing her for ten minutes when Gideon joined him. He whistled to Kit Kat, who pranced over to where he waited. Gideon spoke softly to the horse, taking the time to stroke the patch between her ears before he began her grooming. They worked side by side for a while in the shade of the barn, but Aaron knew that Gideon wasn't grooming his young mare because she needed it. Eunice took care of the horses while they were working at the market. Not that Kit Kat or Misty were complaining about extra attention.

Still, Gideon had joined him for a reason.

"Might as well spill it. I know you'd rather be inside with Becca."

Gideon's laugh was deep, full, genuine. "I like that about you, Aaron. You say what's on your mind."

"It isn't always a *gut* thing."

"I can imagine." Gideon moved to the other side of his mare so that now they were facing one another—

two mares between them. "Now would be a *gut* time to do that…say what's on your mind."

Aaron instinctively shook his head, but he didn't speak.

"You're thinking I can't possibly understand, but remember, I didn't grow up here either."

"You didn't have a father like mine."

"True. My parents had nine children though, so it wasn't as if there was a lot of time or attention to go around." He held up a hand to stop any protest that Aaron might make. "I'm not criticizing them. They provided a roof over my head and three meals a day, but life in Texas…it's very different from life here. When I first arrived in Shipshe, I felt as if I'd stepped off the bus into a story book. It was hard for me to imagine living this way."

He shook his head, swapped out the brush for the comb and began grooming Kit Kat's mane.

"I was the middle of nine children, so I didn't really fit in with the older group or the younger group. Plus—" he shrugged "—I was different."

In spite of himself, Aaron was curious. "How so?"

"I became something of a loner. As the others began marrying, I decided that probably wouldn't happen for me. I convinced myself that I didn't care. Then my parents arranged for me to come here, to work for Amos, and I was not happy about that."

Aaron smiled. "Someone mentioned things were strained between you and Becca at first."

"An understatement. She needed me to believe assistant manager was the best job in the world so she could get out of Shipshe. By the time I came around to her way of thinking, I'd fallen *in lieb*, and she was gone."

"To the mission work."

Gideon nodded, then changed the subject. "You have feelings for Bethany."

"What makes you say that?"

Gideon chuckled. "It's fairly obvious."

How was that possible? He spent all of his energy trying not to show his feelings, trying to put as much space between them as possible. It was exhausting. That thought caught him by surprise. He was more drained from hiding his feelings than he was from the day's work.

"I suspect you won't have much success with denying how you feel about her."

Aaron put up the horse brush, pulled a peppermint from his pocket and offered it to Misty. She took it from the palm of his hand ever so gently, snickering as she did so.

"Why is that?"

"Because the feelings remain, whether you give voice to them or not. Sometimes burying them has the opposite effect—makes them even stronger."

"I do care for Bethany, but my family situation isn't going to change. Sure, we'll rebuild. The church will show up, and if anything, our home will be better than before—the structure, the building itself. But my family? It will be the same. The situation with my *dat*, there isn't really a cure for that, for him."

"And that's your job—to take care of your parents?"

"If Ethan and I don't, who will?"

Gideon offered a carrot to Kit Kat, then another to Oreo, who had been standing by watching. Peanut pushed her way in, and both Gideon and Aaron laughed. It felt strange—to express any emotion other than exhaustion.

Peanut and Oreo didn't need grooming any more than the other two mares. They took the carrots though and crunched happily.

"It's *gut* to care about your family, Aaron. That's admirable. It really is, but maybe the burden of your father isn't yours to carry."

"I don't know what that means."

Instead of answering, Gideon proceeded to shut up the barn for the evening. Aaron followed him as they closed and latched the doors, made sure no lanterns were glowing, carefully did a last check of everything before walking toward the house.

Gideon reached out and touched his arm when they were halfway between the barn and the house. When Aaron had stopped, Gideon nodded toward the house. It looked like a tableau…lamplight glowing in the windows, laughter drifting through the screen door, even the old dog Gizmo lying on the porch.

"All of those people in that house care about you, Aaron. It seems to me that to ignore that is to take a blessing from the Lord and toss it in the rubbish bin. That certainly isn't what He would want you to do."

"But…"

"I don't know the answers you are searching for. I won't pretend to understand what you're going through or what lies ahead. But I do understand that you are now a part of a very special group of people… That fact will remain whether you return the kindness or not."

"And Bethany?" The two words scratched their way out of his throat. He had missed her so much, missed her even though she was sleeping in a room not far from his, eating at the same table, working at the same place.

"Bethany is a woman who knows her own mind and,

I suspect, her own heart. Maybe you should trust that. Maybe you should attend to your own life, and allow your parents to attend to theirs."

When Gideon and Aaron walked back into the house, Bethany understood that something had changed. Instead of saying good night and going straight to his room, Aaron walked over to the chessboard and dared Eunice to trounce him as she had Sarah.

"I will gladly give up my place at this board." Sarah pushed back her chair and motioned for Gideon to take it. "I only seem to get worse."

"Challenge accepted." Eunice began moving the chess pieces back into place.

Forty minutes later, when Ada declared, "I need to get to bed for my ten winks," Aaron laughed with everyone else.

"It wouldn't be so funny if she was *trying* to get the sayings wrong," Eunice explained in a mock whisper. "She always has a reason why her version is the correct one."

"In this case, I am correct. Why would I need forty winks? That doesn't even make sense. Ten winks is bound to be enough for anyone."

But it was as they were all gathering up their things, heading to bed, that Bethany was absolutely certain something Gideon had said to Aaron had pierced through his thick skull. Aaron stood there with his hands in his pockets, waiting for her to stuff her knitting into her bag.

"I probably shouldn't have tried knitting with one arm still in a cast," she admitted. "I made a real mess of things."

"How so?"

A smile played at the corner of his lips, and her pulse did a double tap.

"Well, I knitted where I should have purled, purled where I should have knitted, and I'm fairly sure I dropped a few stitches."

"I have no idea what any of that means."

"Unless you plan on taking up knitting, I suppose you don't need to know what it means."

"Excellent point."

They walked up the stairs slowly, walking side by side. When they reached the upstairs hall, he put his hand on her elbow, waited until she looked at him and said, "Good night, Beth."

It wasn't a lot.

But it was something.

At least he was speaking to her again.

Things between them continued to improve throughout the week. He stopped avoiding her at work. They even resumed their morning walks through the RV park, followed by coffee and tea in the office.

He didn't kiss her.

He didn't mention anything about their relationship or the lack of such. But something in his manner was a little bit lighter.

This Sunday was a Visiting Sunday. Her *dat* had invited a few families over for luncheon—Nathan and Luke, the Lapps and Aaron's *mamm*, and Bishop Ezekiel. It was Nathan's last Sunday in Shipshe. He would be moving to live with family in Sugar Creek, Ohio. Luke would remain at Nathan's place until the new owners took over, which would be in six weeks. It still hadn't been decided where he would live after that. Perhaps, he would go back to Texas. Gideon hadn't shared a lot about Luke's situation, but it was rather obvious that Shipshe hadn't been the cure for whatever ailed him.

Aaron walked up behind Bethany as she was washing the lunch dishes. "You're going to get pruney hands doing that." His voice was low and husky, his breath on her neck.

She nearly jumped out of her apron. "Dishes need washing all the same. Unless you'd like to do it?"

She was teasing, but Aaron was already rolling up his sleeves. "I'll wash. You dry."

They talked about crops, summertime and who was dating whom at the market—nothing terribly important. It wasn't what they talked about that raised her spirits. It was the camaraderie, and she felt something more than the nervousness and butterflies when he had kissed her. It seemed to her that she felt something deeper forming between them. Bethany could envision doing this for the rest of her life—standing at the kitchen window, cleaning the dishes with Aaron. She wanted to deny how strong her feelings were for him, but since he'd moved in, she'd realized how foolish that would be.

She did care about him.

That seemed independent of how he felt about her.

She washed the last plate. He dried it. There was nothing else to do in the kitchen. She supposed it was time to rejoin the group outside and be a polite host.

"Would you like to go for a walk?"

She stumbled backward in mock surprise and placed a hand to her chest. "Wait. You're inviting me to go on one of your very private walks?"

"Privacy might be a bit overrated, and this is, after

all, your home. I suppose you could walk with me if you want."

"I'm astounded."

"Is that a yes?"

"It is."

The calendar had turned to June, and they walked through a day so sunny that Bethany found herself squinting at the blue sky, the green trees, the purple flowers. It almost felt to her as if life had been turned to a brighter setting. Finally, they stopped at the pasture fence to spoil the horses with carrots, then made their way around the fields with crops now knee-high.

"I have a recurring nightmare." Aaron nodded toward the crops. "I'm always lost in a field with crops… tall crops."

He held his hand above his head.

"Can't find your way out?"

"Nope. It's a hopeless maze."

She laughed. "I dream about yarn sometimes. It's usually tangled in a hopeless knot, and I have some project that I urgently need to finish. Or maybe I've lost my knitting needles. You get the idea. It's a variation on the same theme."

"Sometimes…" They'd reached the far side of the field, and he'd stopped, turning to face her. "Sometimes I'm looking for you."

"Ya?"

He nodded. "I have to find you, but I don't know why. And then I look up, and there are storm clouds coming toward us."

"So you rescue me."

"I certainly try to…at least that's how it feels."

She stepped closer, put a hand on both of his shoulders and waited until he made eye contact, and she was certain she had his complete attention. "I don't need rescuing, Aaron. I just need your friendship and maybe..."

He started to speak, but she shook her head.

"Don't interrupt me." Bethany touched his cheek, which might have been a bold thing to do in any other situation, but at the moment, it seemed only natural. "Maybe something more, if you feel the same way about me as I feel about you."

"Of course, I do. How could I not?".

"Well, you do a *gut* impersonation of someone trying to ignore his feelings."

"Gideon let me know that wouldn't work."

"Did he now?" She cocked her head. "I'll have to thank him."

And then Aaron did what she'd been thinking about, dreaming about for some time. He ran his hands up and down her arms, pulled her closer and kissed her.

Then he smiled and reached for her hand.

"I still don't have any answers," he admitted as they walked back toward the house, the guests, his and her family.

"Eh. Answers are overrated."

"Do you think so?"

"I think they can be. Maybe the important thing is that we're going to be asking the questions together."

Chapter Fourteen

On the following Thursday and Friday, Aaron took off two days from the market. He and Ethan needed to pull down the burned portion of their home. The workday to rebuild was scheduled for Saturday.

Bethany wanted to go with him, but she understood that she wouldn't be much help. She knew nothing about tearing down walls. Becca and Gideon, on the other hand, had done that very thing on their honeymoon, which had actually been a mission trip. They both planned to be on-site at the King place to help for most of the two days.

Still, Bethany wished she had a reason to go.

"I won't worry about the RV park because I'll know you will be there handling emergencies." Aaron grinned at her. "That's a bigger help than you can imagine."

They'd taken to sitting on the front porch together after everyone else had gone to bed. They weren't courting, not exactly. She wasn't even sure what that would look like when you lived in the same house. But Aaron wouldn't be living with them much longer.

Late Thursday afternoon, the four of them—Aaron,

Ethan, Becca and Gideon—came home looking dirty, tired and determined. On Friday, they wore grim smiles of satisfaction.

"The site's ready," Aaron explained to Becca. "But it looks pretty sad with a gaping hole in the side of our house."

"A place to rebuild."

"Yeah. Not sure I'll ever look at our kitchen in the same way again."

"Has your *mamm* mentioned what the plan is...going forward?"

"Nope. Not yet. She hasn't said a word, and that is really the deciding question." Aaron leaned forward—elbows on his knees, gaze locked on the floor of the porch. "I can't imagine living with him. I can't see how that would be safe any longer."

Bethany didn't know what to say to that, so she said nothing. She sat with him until he finally raised his head, offered her a sad smile, then reached for her hand. Together they walked back into the house.

The weather on Saturday was picture-perfect. It had been a while since their congregation had needed to schedule a workday at anyone's house, and the people gathering from their church seemed excited to be working on the project.

Some of the men must have arrived at sunrise, because they were already sweating and gratefully accepted large glasses of water. Supplies were neatly laid out, and Benjamin Mast, as the designated site coordinator, directed each volunteer to their assigned task. Benjamin had a loud voice and a pleasant demeanor. It was easy enough to follow his instructions.

Bethany arrived in time for the opening prayer.

"It is *gut* and right that we should work together, *ya*?"

Folks nodded, laughed, then grew serious as Bishop Ezekiel raised his hand. Bethany searched the crowd and saw Aaron and Ethan standing on both sides of their mother. Even across the crowd, Aaron seemed to sense her. He raised his eyes to hers and nodded once.

"It is *gut* and right and proper that we should be the hands and feet of Christ to the world, to our community and to one another."

Everyone stilled, out of respect or perhaps caught up in the beauty and grace of the moment.

"Let us pray."

Tears streamed down Bethany's face as she bowed her head. She couldn't have said why she was weeping—whether it was the tragedy Aaron's family had suffered, the gratitude they were now feeling, the closeness of her community or her own growing devotion to Aaron. Maybe it was all of those things.

Sarah stepped closer on her left, put an arm around her shoulder. Ava reached for her right hand. When Ezekiel finished praying, Eunice and Becca completed the circle of Yoder girls—women now. Words weren't necessary or attempted. Instead, each hugged her, then bustled off to their assigned tasks.

Soon the sound of hammers rang out—sometimes accompanied by a hymn so that their labor was in harmony with their singing. Other times they worked in silence that was broken by conversation or someone's joke—both of which helped to keep the tone of the morning light.

"How did the farmer mend his pants?" Three rings of the hammer, then a pause. "With cabbage patches."

Followed by groans. Bethany had noticed that jokes

were always met with groans as if the listener couldn't believe he'd fallen for the punch line. They were also accompanied with smiles.

When Bethany was young, she remembered the women sitting in a circle and working on some handwork—usually dishcloths or potholders for the person whose home they were building. Some of the older women still did that, but the younger ones—the girls that Bethany had gone to school with—either tended to their young children or worked on the structure with the men.

She didn't exactly see women scrambling across the roof, though she did look up to see the bishop there at one point. Wasn't he too old to be up on a roof? She did see other women hammering in drywall and carrying supplies. Of course, Becca was on a ladder, assigned with the task of installing hurricane joists.

"But we don't have hurricanes," Ava had argued.

"It's just what they're called. They give the structure extra support."

"I think you're pulling my *kapp* string."

At first, Bethany didn't notice the looks thrown her way. Twice she'd taken a pitcher of water and cups to the section where Aaron was working. It was Samuel Mast who gave her the first clue that people were watching her and Aaron.

He'd accepted the cup of water, downed it and handed it back to her. Glancing up at Aaron, he'd said, "We're all very happy for you, Bethany."

"Happy for me?"

"You and Aaron."

"Because…?"

"Ah. Not announced yet. My bad." He pantomimed buttoning his lip. "Still happy for you though."

And then he scampered back up the ladder, leaving Bethany to wonder what was happening. What had he heard? What were people saying? Though truthfully, she didn't care what people were saying. Aaron's home was being rebuilt. He and Ethan would be able to resume their plan to help their parents save the family farm. Those things were what mattered.

She thought she was doing a pretty good job of keeping her romantic feelings for Aaron to herself. Then Esther, Aaron's *mamm*, asked if they could speak privately.

Bethany's eyes widened. "*Ya.* Sure."

Had she done something wrong?

Was Esther worried that her son wasn't ready for a relationship?

They walked away from the house and toward the barn. From there it was easier to see all that was being done—the swarm of men and women who were working together to rebuild the damage wrought by Aaron's *dat*. As they watched, Benjamin called out to the crew on the south side of the kitchen, "Positions. Steady. On my count—one to lift, two to raise, three to put it in its place."

There was a cheer as the wall that had been framed on the ground was lifted into place with ropes and the strength of a dozen men. Three younger men scrambled up onto ladders. Three others hung over from the top. The sound of hammering again rang out, and then it was done. The wall was securely fastened to the structure, and the placing of drywall on the inside and siding on the outside could begin.

"Building a house is like building a home, *ya*?"

Bethany turned to study Esther. She didn't know her well. She was slight. Aaron had mentioned that she was only forty-three years old, but her eyes belied that. The strain of her life was evident in the dark circles.

Bethany realized that she respected this woman and the way she had held her family together. She wanted to know her better. This was the mother of the man that Bethany loved. Had Esther ever wanted a *doschder*? Would she welcome or resent Bethany if things between her and Aaron became serious?

"I remember being young and feeling as you and Aaron do."

"How did you—"

"Aaron hasn't said anything, if that's what you're asking. But a *mamm* can tell. I expect that anyone can tell by the way you two look at one another."

"It's not...that is, he hasn't..."

Esther waited patiently, and wasn't that a point in her favor?

Bethany swallowed and tried again. "I care for Aaron, but I'm not certain that he feels the same."

Esther still didn't speak, but her eyebrows arched as if she knew there were more to the story than that.

"I think he does, but...he seems to be waiting on something."

Now Esther nodded in understanding. "Aaron and Ethan are *gut* sons. Perhaps they had to grow up faster than most because of their *dat*'s illness. I sometimes feel bad about that, but then I remember that *Gotte* has promised plans that will give us hope and a future."

"I'm familiar with the verse, but I'm not sure what you mean."

Ester motioned toward a bench in front of the barn,

and they both sat on it. The sun felt like a kiss on Bethany's skin.

"When I married Zackary, or even before that…when I first fell *in lieb* as you are now… I had no idea what my future would be like." Her gaze drifted to the distant horizon and she slowly shook her head. "If I had known, I might not have had the courage to move forward."

She brought her attention back to Bethany.

"But I believe that *Gotte* has had a plan—a *gut* plan—all along, through all the tragedies, even through this fire. Look at how much closer it has brought our two families."

That was true. Ethan now felt like a *bruder*, or at the very least a cousin. And Aaron…well, living together had made ignoring each other—ignoring their feelings—impossible. If the fire hadn't happened, they might have taken a very long time to begin to trust one another. They might have never learned that important lesson.

"*Gotte* could have made me barren, but he didn't." Now Esther's face broke into a smile.

The smile gentled the lines on her face. Bethany thought she could see something of the young woman who had fallen *in lieb* so very long ago.

"Gotte gave me two sons—two *gut* sons. I'm grateful for that, and I wouldn't exchange all the heartache of the past twenty-five years for a peaceful life if it meant that I wouldn't have Ethan and Aaron to add value and meaning to my days."

She stood, seemingly finished with what she wanted to say, so Bethany stood too. Before they started back though, Esther put a hand on Bethany's arm. "I am grateful that you care for my son."

Bethany nodded mutely and then stood frozen to

the spot as Esther raised a hand in greeting to one of the women who was just exiting her buggy. She hurried off to help the woman carry a casserole and bag of groceries, leaving Bethany to wonder about what had just happened.

Had Esther given her blessing?

But Aaron hadn't even said he loved her yet. She hadn't said it to him either. Should she? Or should she wait? It was the age-old question posed in so many romance books, and yes, she had read a few of those in her younger years. But this wasn't a story. It was her life.

Part of her wanted to proceed with caution.

Another part wanted to jump in with reckless abandon.

On the day that his parents' house was rebuilt, Aaron fell in love. Maybe he'd been falling all along, and he hadn't realized it. One thing was for certain. He couldn't imagine a future without Bethany in it, and she seemed to feel the same way. So what was holding him back?

He spent the next week chewing on that answer.

Work was busy, so that should have helped.

But it didn't.

Because everywhere he turned, he encountered Bethany—in the office, at church, even at her home. His parents' house was very nearly done—everything except the finishing touches—but he and Ethan were still staying at the Yoder place. It was easier to complete the work on their house without anyone living in it. So Aaron went to the RV park each day, put in a solid eight hours, then rode his bike to their home on Huckleberry Lane. By the time he arrived there, Ethan was finished in the fields, and they tackled a project inside of the house. Most evenings, he wasn't back at the Yoder place until the sun had already set.

Every single night, Sarah set back food for them.

Every single night, Ada made them laugh, and Eunice discussed some new invention.

At least once each evening, he saw Gideon and Becca steal a quick kiss or hold hands or merely walk across the fields together.

And always, Bethany was there, some needlework in her hands, a smile on her face, ready to hear about his day.

Each evening, he crawled into his bed—exhausted but filled with the satisfaction of having put in a good day's work. That wasn't his last thought before drifting off though. He fell asleep realizing he was a little more in love with Bethany than he had been the day before.

So what was holding him back?

Why didn't he ask her to marry him?

He knew part of the answer, knew that it had something to do with his father, but the problem was so big and had been with him for so long that he didn't know how to get his arms around it. Instead, he'd rise early the next day and go through the same set of motions. And he might have continued that way until Bethany gave up on him or they were both old and gray and still courting.

But fate or chance or God intervened.

Since the market had officially opened for the season, most workers had switched their days to Tuesday through Saturday, as had he and Bethany. Which meant that he had church on Sunday and could work on finishing his parents' house all day Monday.

He and Aaron had tackled the kitchen…installing

new cabinets and countertops, which had been provided through the benevolence fund. They also had a new-to-them gas refrigerator and gas stove donated by someone who was upgrading their own place. Both had been cleaned until they shone by the person donating them. Aaron didn't know who. It didn't matter. Their entire church had provided all that was necessary to rebuild their home.

He felt indebted to them all.

He felt grateful to them all.

They'd finished installing everything and were moving in a small kitchen table that had been donated when they were interrupted by the clatter of buggy wheels.

Ethan wiggled his eyebrows. "Bethany?"

"*Nein*. She was going to get her cast off this afternoon."

They walked out onto the porch surprised to hear their *mamm* calling out "Whoa, girl." She pulled up on the reins, set the brake and hopped out of the Lapps's buggy. She was holding a letter-sized envelope, which she tucked under her arm as she walked toward them.

"*Mamm* looks *gut*," Ethan said.

"Being away from here seems to have given her some of her energy back, which seems to have helped her." Later, Aaron would wonder why he'd said that, if some deep-seated instinct had warned him that something was about to change.

Esther hugged both Aaron and Ethan, then they walked her through the house pointing out what had been done and what there still was to do.

"You boys—what am I saying? You're both men now, and you've done a fine job here." She nodded her head toward the kitchen table. "Sit with me for a minute?"

"Sure." Ethan glanced at Aaron, who shrugged. "I have to warn you, those cabinets are empty...there's not so much as a tin of tea."

"That's all right. I just wanted to talk with you both—privately."

She placed the envelope on the table, hung her purse strap over the back of the chair and sat. Aaron realized that Ethan was right. She did look *gut*. She looked different. He steeled himself for what she was about to say.

Esther smiled, reached out and patted his hand. "No need to stiffen your shoulders. I believe you'll find this to be *gut* news."

Now he was really worried, but he forced his shoulders down and attempted to smile back at her.

"Your *dat* and I have made a decision. We're moving to Sarasota. We're going to live with my parents."

She waited then, allowed space for her announcement to settle in. Neither Aaron nor Ethan said a word. They waited. It seemed to Aaron that they'd spent their entire life waiting.

"As you may both realize, my relationship with my parents has been strained for some time. Actually, since the day I went against their advice and married your *dat*. Over the years, we have exchanged occasional letters, but they were filled with mundane, ordinary details. We never...we never spoke of the struggles in my marriage."

"Why?" The word seemed to pop out of Aaron's mouth against his own volition.

"Once you decide to hold on to a thing, to keep it to yourself, it becomes difficult to share." She rested her eyes on him, and Aaron saw in that gaze all of her love and regrets and years of struggle. He also saw something else though. Something new that he couldn't quite name.

"Let that be a lesson to you both. Secrets can build walls between you and those you love. You might tell yourself that you're doing it for them, but in the end, it's a cowardice on your own part. At least it was on mine."

"You did the best you could, *Mamm*." Ethan sat back and folded his arms. "We won't be judging you for that. No one should."

She cocked her head, smiled and nodded. "After the fire though, something in me broke. Of course, I've always known that living with your *dat* was difficult, a burden...but I told myself that we all have burdens. I told myself that it was no more than I deserved."

Her elbows propped on the table, she rubbed her fingertips against her forehead, and in that moment, Aaron realized how difficult this was for her. He wanted to stop her, to tell her that she didn't have to explain a thing, but before he could, she sat up straighter and continued.

"The fire had a way of clarifying my thinking...or perhaps it was living with Ben and Martha." She smiled now, and it was a clear, unburdened thing. "Martha and I were young scholars together. Over the years, we'd drifted apart...*nein*. That's not right. I'd stepped away from all my relationships. Being with her again, being with them and seeing how a normal family lives opened my eyes."

She turned the envelope over, lifted the flap and pulled out a small stack of papers. Aaron could only see that they were typed and that they looked official.

"Last week, I went to your *dat* and told him that I was moving back to Sarasota, and that I would like him to go with me."

"And he was okay with that?" Ethan shook his head

in surprise. "He's always insisted on staying here, even when he couldn't make the place work."

"It's true. He resisted the idea at first, but in the end, he's come around to seeing the wisdom in moving and making a fresh start. Neither of us are too old for that. We have agreed that a change will do him *gut*. Here…" She glanced around the house, surveyed the newly painted walls, the shining used appliances. "Here we have a lot of history. It's too easy for your *dat* to fall into his old ways. And I need other adults to help me care for him, help me keep him on the right path."

"I don't understand. You're both moving?" Ethan's brow was furrowed with concern. "We're all moving?"

"*Nein*. Just me and your *dat*. And we want to give the farm to both of you—if you'll have it." She tapped the papers. "You've certainly put in the work, and it's your home."

"*Mamm*, you don't have to do that." Aaron was having trouble keeping up with all that she was saying.

"I know I don't have to. Actually, it was your *dat*'s idea to put the deed in your name. It will be official, though you'll have to pay us for it to be official on the county records." A smile wreathed her face. "The sum of one dollar is sufficient."

"The farm will be ours?" Ethan stood, walked to the window, stared out over the fields, then sat back down at the table.

"Not free and clear. There will be the loan to pay— you already know about that. It will take hard work, but I think after watching you two these past weeks that you have a real chance of making a go of it here. And your *dat* and I have a chance of doing well in Sarasota. Of course, we would like you to come and visit."

They spent another twenty minutes going over details and timetables, then they stood and walked her to the buggy.

Ethan hugged her. "I best go and see to Misty. We'll talk again, before you leave."

Which left Aaron standing there trying to wrap his mind around what had just happened and how he felt about it. His *mamm* reached up and touched his face. "You're a *gut* man, Aaron. If I'm not mistaken, you've become very close to Bethany...perhaps, you are even *in lieb*?"

Aaron felt the blush crawl up his neck, but he nodded.

He was in love with Bethany. Of course he was.

She put her arms around him, hugged him to her, and then kissed his cheek. "I'm happy for you. Bethany is a lovely girl. Have you asked her yet?"

"Nein."

"What are you waiting for?"

He shrugged, but she was already answering. "I suspect you were afraid of asking her to take up a life in your *dat*'s shadow."

Aaron swallowed a lump in his throat. "She's strong, but I couldn't ask... It didn't seem right to..."

She squeezed his arm, then climbed into the buggy. He shut the door and stood there, arms propped on the open window.

"Love bears all things, Son, believes all things, hopes all things and endures all things." She smiled brightly, and he realized that she really had changed, and it was possible that the changes in her would bring about changes in his father. At least she was trying something different. She wasn't giving up on Aaron's *dat*, but she was forcing him to accept the consequences of his actions.

"Speak to Bethany. Tell her what's on your heart."

And then she was gone, leaving Aaron standing in the middle of a farm that had just become his—well, half his. He felt that he was about to step over a threshold and into a new life, and he wanted to do so with Bethany.

There was only one thing stopping him.

The question was…what was he willing to do about it?

Chapter Fifteen

It was three days later before Aaron had a chance to speak privately with Bethany's *dat*. He could have gone to Amos's office, but what he wanted to talk about was too personal for that. Best to wait for the right time and the right place—which happened when Amos asked him to walk to the back pasture and check the crops with him.

Aaron was no expert in sorghum. It would have made more sense for Amos to ask Gideon or Ethan, but he didn't. He clapped a hand on Aaron's shoulder and asked, "Walk with me to check the sorghum?"

A look passed from Sarah to Becca to Bethany—a look Aaron couldn't quite read.

"It'll be an hour before dinner." Sarah was smiling broadly. "Take your time."

Which was also suspicious, as they usually ate promptly at six o'clock, and the clock above the stove read twenty minutes before. Aaron shrugged and reached for his hat. At first, they walked in silence. The sun dipped toward the horizon. Its rays spilling across the field gave the scene in front of him a storybook quality. The sorghum was coming in nicely, but Aaron suspected that Amos knew that.

When they'd reached the far end of the field, Amos nodded toward a bench placed underneath a tree. Aaron thought he'd seen most of the Yoder farm, but he'd never seen that bench.

"Put this here for my *fraa* when Sarah was a babe. Lydia wanted time away from the house. I can still see them sitting here in my mind—Sarah crawling on that quilt that's across the back of the couch now. Lydia enjoying the fresh air, the sunshine and her family."

Aaron only nodded, unsure exactly how to respond.

"Family is important, *ya*?"

"I think so."

Amos sat on the bench and waited for Aaron to join him. "Seems to me that you've had something on your mind, son."

And it was that word, *son*, which opened the flood of words that had been trapped somewhere between Aaron's heart and his voice. He sat next to Amos and blurted out, "I love Bethany."

"That's *gut* to hear. Bethany seems to care for you as well."

Aaron dared to look at Amos then and was surprised to see the man smiling.

"Wouldn't it worry you for her to marry me?"

"Should I be worried?"

His throat suddenly tight, Aaron simply nodded.

"I'm guessing that you're referring to your *dat*'s condition. Possibly you've decided in your mind that your parents' place wouldn't be a safe environment to raise a family, but you're always welcome to live here, Aaron." He motioned back toward the house. "We could add on a room, or even build another home. It's what Gideon and Becca plan to do."

"That's not the problem. It was... I mean, I was worried about that very thing, but now my parents are moving to Sarasota, so it's not an issue. They could come back, I suppose, but somehow, I think that this move—for them—is permanent." He went on to explain how his *mamm* had given the farm to them for the sum of one dollar. "Of course, it comes with debt, but Ethan and I have a *gut* plan for paying that off in the next year—eighteen months at the most."

"So, it's something else that's bothering you—something other than where you would live."

Aaron nodded, and perhaps it was the fact that Amos waited—not pushing, not prying—that helped Aaron to find the words. "What if I'm like him?"

It was the question that circled his mind constantly, the fear that kept him awake at night. It was the single thing standing between the life he had and the life he dreamed of having.

Amos didn't answer immediately. He studied Aaron, then stared out over the sorghum field, a soft green in the afternoon's last light. "Being a farmer isn't for everyone. It can be a worrisome thing. Will there be enough rain? Will there be too much rain? Will some insects attack the new growth? Will prices fall before the crops are harvested?"

"Okay. I get it." Aaron nodded his head in understanding. "You're telling me that everything has a risk, and I'm okay with that. I'm okay for me, but Bethany... she deserves more certainty in life."

"In what way?"

"She deserves a husband she can count on—who will

always be there for her, who will support her in every aspect of her life. My *dat* hasn't done that for my *mamm*. Perhaps he can't, but regardless the reason, she has had to carry most burdens alone. I want Bethany to have a long and *wunderbaar* life, and I want her burdens to be shared by those she loves."

Amos smiled, and in that smile was an ache and a tenderness that caught Aaron by surprise. "I wanted the same for my Lydia. *Gotte* had other plans."

"How can it be *Gotte*'s plan for her to die so young, die while your girls were still babes?"

If Amos was offended by Aaron's words, by his questioning the will of *Gotte*, he didn't show it. Instead, he said, "I asked the same question for many years. Raising five girls on my own…it seemed an insurmountable task."

"Why did you never remarry?"

Amos shrugged. "I suppose I never met the right woman. My point is that Lydia was very happy for the time she was allotted."

"And you?"

"I've had a *gut* life. For sure and certain, it wasn't the life I envisioned, but I wouldn't do a thing differently, because from that life *Gotte* gave me five beautiful *doschdern*."

"You're telling me to trust."

"I'm saying that we can't always know, and so we pray, we care for one another, we do the best we can."

"How do I know I'm doing my best?"

"You'll know, and if not, I'll be there to guide you— as will Bethany's *schweschdern* and Gideon."

Misery washed over Aaron. He propped his elbows on his knees and dropped his head into his hands. "If

I knew that I had *dat*'s disease, I would walk away. I wouldn't ask Bethany to go through such a life."

"Perhaps, that would be Beth's decision."

"Maybe." He sat up straighter and met Amos's gaze. "I've seen what such a decision has done to my *mamm* though. I know firsthand what it's done to me and Ethan."

Round and round the thoughts and doubts and questions went in his head.

Trust?

Or sacrifice what he wanted so that Bethany could have a normal life—a *gut* life?

"Have you talked to his doctors?"

"What?"

"Have you talked to your *dat*'s doctors? Explained your concerns to them? I'm no expert on *Englisch* medicine, though I have some experience from my *fraa*'s cancer. It seemed to me then that these doctors have made it their life's purpose to treat such diseases. Perhaps they can shed some light on the likelihood that you inherited your *dat*'s bipolar disorder."

Aaron looked at Amos in appreciation. Amos didn't shy away from calling the disease what it was. He didn't tell Aaron to pray more fervently—though he had done quite a bit of that over the last few weeks, actually over the last few years. Instead, Amos suggested something so logical that it nearly knocked Aaron off the bench.

See his *dat*'s doctors. Ask them his questions.

"I hadn't thought of that. Amos, that's a great idea. That's genius."

"Ah. Well, they say if you want wisdom, seek an old man's counsel."

"Or woman's."

"Indeed."

Aaron hopped up, walked to the edge of the field, then walked back. "I'll do it. I'll make an appointment and go and talk to them."

"Fine idea."

The last question that Aaron needed to answer was whether he would ask Bethany to go with him, or tell her what he learned from the doctor after the fact.

It was the following Monday, four days after Aaron had spoken with Bethany's *dat*. It had taken that long to work things out in his mind and then make an appointment with his *dat*'s doctors. He'd come home, eaten dinner without so much as saying a word, then asked her to go to the porch with him. There, he'd told her how much he cared for her. He'd said that he had decided to see his *dat*'s doctors…that it might be important to their future. Did she want to go? He'd made the appointment for the next day.

Of course, she wanted to go.

She wanted to be by Aaron's side no matter what he went through, and she understood that this was a very big step for him. She understood that his *dat*'s condition was a constant worry on his mind. If the doctor could ease some of that worry, she was all for taking the afternoon off and making the visit.

Since the medical center was in Middlebury, they hired an *Englisch* driver to take them.

"It was nice of Eunice to cover for us at the office." Aaron reached out and placed his hand over Bethany's.

"*Ya*. We'll probably come back to find that she's created a solar sprinkler system for your bed of flowers."

"Not a bad idea, actually."

The medical center wasn't what she'd expected. She'd thought it would be like the small hospital in Goshen, where her *dat* had gone after his heart attack—long halls, fluorescent lights and the smell of disinfectant. The medical center in Middlebury was quite different. It looked more like a nice home for elderly folks.

The grounds around the building were well kept, sporting large trees and brimming with spring flowers. It helped that the weather was sunny and warm. It was a beautiful June day, and perhaps the day that Aaron would find some answers. Once inside, she found the lighting to be softer—a good deal of it coming from the large windows and scattered lamps. The floors were covered with rugs. The chairs looked like what you would find in a home, and the smell of the place reminded her of summer.

A Mennonite woman at the information desk explained that the doctors' offices were located in the north wing. They found the door labeled "Doctor Rodriguez," then paused. Aaron pulled in a deep breath and squared his shoulders, as if he were Daniel himself walking into the lion's den. Bethany reached for his hand, held it and didn't let it go. He smiled at her, squeezed her hand back, and they walked into the office.

After waiting about twenty minutes, a young woman in lavender nursing scrubs led them down a short hall to Dr. Rodriguez's office. He rose to shake their hands. Dr. Rodriguez was middle-aged with black hair just beginning to turn gray. He was slight, approximately Bethany's height and wore wire-rim glasses. Those glasses helped Bethany to relax. They reminded her of her *dat*. Or perhaps the kind look he gave them reminded her of her *dat*. Regardless, she felt immediately at ease.

Aaron and Bethany introduced themselves.

"When you scheduled your appointment, you said you wanted to discuss your father's condition. Since that time, we have received a release from your father saying that we can share his personal records with you." Dr. Rodriguez tapped a folder on his desk, but he didn't open it. "I've been working with your father personally since his initial visit. What would you like to know?"

Aaron tossed a nervous look Bethany's way, and she attempted to give him a reassuring smile.

"I'd like to know if there's a chance that I have his disorder."

Dr. Rodriguez cocked his head to the side, waiting for more.

"Is there a test you can do? Like they do for people who might have cancer?"

Now Dr. Rodriguez took off his glasses, polished them and then donned them again. "Unfortunately, we don't yet have a genetic test for what your father suffers from. It's a bit more complicated than testing for a single inherited gene mutation. How well do you understand your father's condition?"

"I know it's called bipolar disorder and that it includes…" He raised his hand high, then dropped it.

"Manic episodes followed by depressive episodes— that's exactly right. Our goal here—" now Dr. Rodriguez raised his hand, dropped it low, and brought it back to somewhere in the middle "—is to even that out. To smooth out the highs and lows. But to your original question…"

He sat back, interlaced his fingers, and tapped his thumbs together. "Researchers are certain there is a genetic link, but it's complicated. No one gene seems responsible for the condition. Rather, it appears to be a combination of genetic and environmental or behavioral factors. Because of that, for children of someone with bipolar disorder, the absolute risk is not high."

"I don't understand."

"If one or both of your parents are bipolar, it doesn't necessarily follow that you will be."

"Okay." Aaron glanced at Bethany again. "That's *gut*, right?"

"It should offer you some measure of reassurance. Let's talk about your medical history. Have you experienced any stressful life events?"

"Living with my *dat* was a stressful life event."

"Right." Now Dr. Rodriguez opened the file, read something, and closed it. "The recent fire was no doubt traumatic."

"It was."

"How did you respond to that?"

"Our church helped provide materials to rebuild. While that was happening, I stayed with Bethany's family—both my *bruder* and I did. A workday was scheduled, and the damaged portion of our home was demolished then rebuilt. All that's left is for Ethan and I to finish the last bits to make our home livable again."

Dr. Rodriguez was nodding his head as Aaron spoke. "Sounds as if you handled things well. It's also a good sign that you have a supportive community."

"*Ya*. It's the Amish way to help one another."

Dr. Rodriguez tapped his fingers against the file. "Any abrupt changes in your sleep patterns?"

"*Nein*. I'm so tired at the end of the day that I usually fall asleep as my head is hitting the pillow."

"And have you experienced any chronic medical illnesses?"

"I'm not sure what that is exactly, but I'm healthy as an ox."

"Have you experienced any highs and lows similar to your father's?"

"Nein."

Now Dr. Rodriguez sat up, placed both hands on the table and looked first at Bethany then Aaron. "Is it safe to assume that you two are considering a life together?"

Bethany found herself nodding even before she glanced at Aaron to see his response. He was nodding too. Aaron had not asked her to marry him, but were they both thinking about it? Yes. They were.

"Do you have any questions for me, Bethany?"

"I'm here to support Aaron, and—" she sat up straighter "—I'd like to know what I can do to help."

Dr. Rodriguez smiled broadly. "The fact that you're willing and eager to provide whatever assistance he needs and that you're here right now—both are huge benefits to Aaron. As to what you can do—" He spread his hand out, palms up. "Watch for any of the symptoms I just mentioned. Have an open dialogue with Aaron about how he's feeling and also how you're feeling."

"Of course. *Ya.* Those are *gut* suggestions."

"Should your relationship with Aaron become more…" He smiled broadly. "Should it become official, then your role would be even more fundamental to his health. In the future, should Aaron show symptoms of bipolar disorder, it would be very important for you to join a support group."

She dared to glance at Aaron again. He was watching her with such tenderness that tears sprang to her eyes and her throat tightened. She didn't trust her voice, so she nodded that she understood.

"I wish that more young people would come to see me about their concerns. Aaron, the fact that you were willing to do so tells me that you're being vigilant about monitoring your health. That's an important thing. Denial is not our friend here."

"What does that mean?"

"It means that based on your answers, you don't display any of the symptoms for bipolar disorder now. While there is a genetic component to the disease, there are also lifestyle and environmental components. Anxiety disorder, panic attacks, ADHD and substance abuse all can be contributing factors."

"I don't have or do any of those things."

Dr. Rodriguez was smiling again now. "That's good, Aaron. The best thing that you can do to guard against this disease is take care of yourself. Be mindful of your habits. Develop normal sleep patterns, stick to a healthy diet, exercise regularly and avoid alcohol and drugs… the same things that we do to ward off many other diseases."

He stood and shook their hands.

"*Danki* for answering my questions."

"Anytime." They were nearly to the door when Dr. Rodriguez called them back. "Your father has made great progress here, despite the fire at your home. I believe that his plan to move to Sarasota is a good one, and I've referred him to a colleague in the area. Your father will have a care team to look after him. There's every reason to be optimistic about his overall condition."

Bethany wondered if Aaron had ever heard those words before. He didn't respond. Instead, he nodded, reached for her hand, and together they walked down the hall toward the front door of the building. She thought they'd head straight for the *Englisch* car that had picked them up. Aaron had told the man to give them an hour, and they weren't inside the medical center quite that long. Instead of looking toward the parking lot though, once they were outside, Aaron pulled her over to a bench under a maple tree.

She waited, watching him, allowing him the time to sort through his feelings. Finally, he met her gaze. "I'm glad you came with me."

"I always want to support you, Aaron."

"And that helps. It does. But just as importantly, I wanted you to hear Dr. Rodriguez's answers for yourself. I was afraid that I might interpret his words the way I wanted to hear them."

She nodded as if she understood, and maybe she did—a little.

"You were worried that if we—"

"Married..." He stared at their hands, fingers still entwined, unable or unwilling to give voice to his fears.

"You were worried that if we married, you might learn later that you have bipolar disorder."

"Exactly."

"But I would love you regardless, Aaron. I don't love you because you're healthy. I love you because you're you."

"Right. And I feel the same about you, but I couldn't... I wouldn't..."

She could have finished the sentences for him, but in the deep recesses of Bethany's heart, she understood that he needed to say these things. He needed to work out his own fears and hopes and longings.

"I couldn't put you through what my *mamm* has been through. I wouldn't ever forgive myself."

"You know, I wouldn't want to put you through what my *dat* has been through."

"What do you mean?"

"Cancer can be hereditary. You're at as much risk for heartbreak as I am. Everyone's life is uncertain, Aaron."

"You sound like your *dat*." He smiled when he said that, so Bethany assumed it was a *gut* thing. Then more softly, he added, "Tell me what you heard Dr. Rodriguez say."

"Let's see." She stood, walked toward the tree and placed her hands against its bark. The tree felt solid. She liked that about trees. And she liked it about the man waiting in front of her. He was solid and dependable and caring. Those thoughts caused a smile to tug at her lips even as she turned, leaned her back against the tree and ticked off the doctor's main points. "Bipolar disorder could be genetic. No test for that yet. You don't have any of the symptoms. And there are things we can do that will help protect you against it."

"I like that you said *we*."

"Good sleep, regular exercise, healthy diet...sounds like the Plain life, *ya*?"

"Don't forget no drugs or alcohol."

"Indeed." Now she was smiling broadly. When he didn't say anything else, she finally pushed just a little. "Was there something you wanted to ask me, Aaron King?"

Now his smile matched hers. He glanced around, seemed to assure himself that they were alone, stood and walked closer. "Indeed, there is."

"Well?"

"Would you marry me, Bethany Yoder?" His voice was tender and the expression on his face held such hope and such wonder. "Would you be my *fraa* and, if *Gotte* is willing, raise a houseful of children with me?"

She tapped a finger against her lips and stared up into the maple tree as if she needed a moment to consider.

Aaron stepped closer so that there was the slightest space between them—no more than a breath. His voice low and urgent, he asked, "Do you love me, Bethany?"

She met his gaze, her heart beating a staccato pattern, her hands sweating slightly and a smile tugging at the corners of her lips. "I do."

"And will you marry me?"

"Yes, Aaron. Yes, I will."

Epilogue

She wore a dress the color of pumpkin spice — a soft, gentle blend of orange and yellow with a matching apron and a new white *kapp*.

He wore black slacks, a white shirt, suspenders, a black hat and a black jacket. He looked like a proper Amish man.

Someone walking by might have thought them to be a typical Amish couple, but Aaron and Bethany both knew that their love for one another was far from typical. The fact that they'd moved on from the first day at the market, when Aaron had tracked mud through Bethany's office, proved that one could never tell what direction love might take you.

They wed under the gazebo on a beautiful Monday in September. Orange, red and yellow chrysanthemums lined the walk, the leaves had turned brilliant shades of gold, and the sky was blue. The market was open through the end of the month, but technically closed on Mondays. You couldn't tell it by the parking area, which was filled with buggies as well as a smattering of cars.

Bethany glanced at the front row—at her *schwe-*

schdern sitting oldest to youngest, with Gideon between Becca and Eunice. At the end of the row sat her *dat* and, next to him, Ethan. He was the only one there to represent Aaron's side of the family, and that was okay. His *mamm* and *dat* were settled in Sarasota, and his *dat* was still on the path to recovery.

Their entire church family was in attendance, as well as all the workers from the market and of course all the residents in their RV park. It made for an unusually large portion of *Englisch* guests, who seemed amused to have to endure two sermons as well as several long hymns before the exchange of vows.

Finally, Bishop Ezekiel cleared his throat and began addressing Bethany and Aaron, who were standing in the center of the gazebo, holding hands, facing one another.

"Aaron King and Bethany Yoder, do you both vow to remain together until death?"

"We do."

Ezekiel nodded and smiled, as if that were the perfect answer—and it was. For Bethany and Aaron, it most certainly was. "Will you both be loyal and care for each other during adversity?"

"We will."

"And during affliction?"

"Yes."

"And during sickness?"

Aaron glanced down at his feet, and when he looked up, Bethany saw tears shining in his eyes. She loved this man more than she would have ever thought possible. She squeezed his hands.

Together, in one voice, they said, "We will."

"*Wunderbaar.*" Ezekiel tucked his Bible under his arm,

and covered their hands with his own. "All assembled here—Amish and *Englisch*, family and friend—and I, as your bishop, wish you the blessing and mercy of God."

Bethany's eyes filled with tears. She heard a ringing in her ears and behind that the shouts of congratulations coming from their family, friends and RV campers. She wanted to laugh, and she was afraid she would cry.

"Go forth in the Lord's name." Ezekiel put his hand on their arms and gently turned them to face their guests. "You are now man and wife."

And weren't those the sweetest words she'd ever heard? Her *dat* had taken off his glasses and was wiping his eyes. Sarah was laughing and saying something to Eunice. Becca and Gideon were looking at each other as if they were the ones who had just married. Ada and Ethan were hugging.

Their family was growing, and Bethany couldn't wait to see what it would become.

* * * * *

Dear Reader,

Have you ever felt like you finally found your niche in life, only to be displaced? Have you wanted to break free from your past, but doubted whether that was actually possible?

Bethany Yoder enjoys working at the Amish market, in the little RV park. She never thought she would, but life is full of surprises. Until she finds Aaron King standing in her office. Aaron is a surprise she does not want in her life. He causes her to feel things—complicated and messy and confusing things. Aaron is struggling with the mighty burden of his family history, and he has no idea how to break free from that. Then he begins to fall for Bethany.

Sometimes dramatic surprises are the very things we need in our lives. Sometimes they are what God uses to show us an even brighter and better future.

I hope you enjoyed reading *Her Amish Adversary*. I welcome comments and letters at vannettachapman@gmail.com.

May we continue "giving thanks always for all things unto God the Father in the name of our Lord Jesus Christ" (Ephesians 5:20).

Blessings,
Vannetta

Get 4 FREE REWARDS!

We'll send you 2 FREE Books plus 2 FREE Mystery Gifts.

FREE Value Over **$20**

Both the **Love Inspired®** and **Love Inspired®** **Suspense** series feature compelling novels filled with inspirational romance, faith, forgiveness and hope.

HARLEQUIN
PLUS

Try the best multimedia
subscription service for romance
readers like you!

Read, Watch and Play.

Experience the easiest way to get
the romance content you crave.

Start your **FREE TRIAL** at
www.harlequinplus.com/freetrial.